TEO AND THE BANYAN TREE

JACOB C. SADLER

AUBERDINE PUBLISHING

Printed in the United States of America

First Printing, 2026

ISBN 979-8-9859095-6-2 *(paperback)*

ISBN 979-8-9859095-7-9 *(ebook)*

Auberdine Publishing
2519 S Shields Street
Suite 1K #612
Fort Collins, CO 80526

For my friend, KJ.

CONTENTS

CERTIFIABLY DEAD

KODA ALWAYS IMAGINED A morgue would be scary. You know—creepy corridors covered in cobwebs, leading to dark rooms full of chrome-colored cabinets. He had envisioned a dim hallway lit by a far-off, fluorescent light. At the end of the hall would be a claustrophobic room. There a single light would flicker, illuminating everything in a pale, ghostly light. Meanwhile, flies would buzz forebodingly above cluttered tables of nasty, faceless things.

Instead, Koda was greeted with coffee breath. The only chrome was in the slightly rusted folding chairs that filled the lobby. The only humming came from a vending machine (and from whoever was currently figuring out that it did not work). The lobby did not smell bad, either. Nothing like he imagined. More like a department store than a morgue.

Koda was right about the fluorescent lights, though. They were everywhere.

People had come and gone all morning. Most were there for reasons other than death. At least, Koda thought so. They were all too badly dressed to be grieving. Not that Koda was all that well-dressed himself. His caseworkers had bought him a pair of ill-fitting slacks and a black, satin button-up. Koda had conveniently lost them this morning. He had no choice but to wear baggy gym shorts and a hoodie.

By noon, the lobby was full. Many people passed the time on their phones, flicking their fingers up and down to look as if they had things to do. Some made small talk with Koda's caseworkers, speaking in short sentences that, according to his English teacher, were not sentences at all. Just subjects without a predicate.

All had business with a single woman behind a thick, glass screen. Koda fancied she was a fortune teller—until he heard her raspy voice. He could practically smell the cigarettes from his seat. However, she must have been important, because she rarely met with anyone in the lobby. For the most part, she just typed and chewed bubble gum. Meanwhile, the lobby grew fuller and fuller (and the vending machine took more and more abuse).

"This is her job?" Koda asked one of his caseworkers.

"Ostensibly," said the male one.

Koda did not know what stencils had to do with his question. He pulled his hood over his head and stretched the fabric over his knees. He dozed off, trying not to dream about his mother and especially not his father. After a while, someone poked him. Like a hermit crab, he emerged from his hoodie. His caseworkers were pointing at the Lady Behind the Glass. "Your turn," they said.

Koda stumbled up, kicking his shoes slightly to wake up his tingly leg. He approached the woman, who slid a paper and a pen through the glass. The pen had a plastic rose taped over the fun, clicky part. The faded dye on the petals made the whole thing look wilted.

"Sign here," said the woman. She was just as interesting to look at up close as she was from afar. For one, her ears were incredibly hairy. Like nests. This made it seem as though she had stuffed little dolls into them. A huge wart also rested on the tip of her nose, making it seem like it was wearing a top hat.

Koda stood on his tiptoes and blinked at the small font before him. Whatever the page was trying to say, it was not doing a very good job. The big words and flowery letters were like another language. "What is it?"

"Certification that you have received your father's ashes."

Koda squinted at the wall of words. "That's it?"

"There's some other information about cause of death. Clerical details, you know?" She blew a bubble of gum that popped on her cheeks.

Adults made no sense. After all, who else would make you sign something to be dead? Koda imagined he was signing a permission slip for a school trip. That stilled his trembling hands and gave him enough strength to scribble his name in the blank space. He handed the document back to the warty woman.

She filed the paper and took out a small, white box. It was held shut by ornate, interlacing ferns. The caseworkers said that had cost extra. "Have a nice day," the administrator said, shoving the urn toward him.

Now between you and me, Koda did *not* want her to have a nice day. In fact, he wanted her to have anything but. However, he had learned that honesty for adults was like spicy foods or milk; they develop an intolerance to it as they age. So, he said nothing. He took his father's urn, gave her a dishonest smile, and walked away.

His caseworkers, or "agents" as they preferred to be called, were waiting near the flickering hallway lights. The older agent was named Burlington; he had a deep voice and did not speak much. His receding hairline made him look like a bird. The younger agent was named Wellington and she was nice enough. Her brown hair was tied neatly in a big bun and she wore dangly hoop earrings.

As for Koda, he was short for his age and had green eyes and long hair. He was rather insecure, and like most boys his age, dealt with those feelings by hiding behind long, swoopy bangs. The caseworkers had insisted he cut his hair, but after a few choice words (which he had learned from his father), they had given up.

"Excited to see your mom, Koda?" Agent Wellington asked.

He shrugged. It seemed stupid to get excited over a person he did not know.

"Don't worry, son," Agent Burlington said. "It's all over. Now you can finally go home."

"Mhm," Koda hummed. He did not hate the agents, but he did not like them either (especially Burlington). He disliked people whose job it was to be nice.

The agents glanced at one another. Burlington frowned, "Look, son. Your mother would have found you sooner, but your father kept moving you. You understand that, right?"

"I'm not your son," Koda quipped.

Burlington licked his lips and made a popping sound with them. "Right you are." He glanced at his feet and cleared his throat a few times.

Wellington looked at her watch. She put a supportive hand on the other agent's shoulder. "Why don't you head home, Charlie?"

Burlington asked in that voice grownups use when they need to sound polite but are perfectly content with the suggestion. "Are you sure?"

"Yep. I insist," Wellington smiled.

Burlington stuttered a few remarks to make it seem like he did not want to go. Then, he shrugged at Koda and smiled, "You take care of yourself, okay?"

The boy glared, "Who else is going to?"

Burlington could not form a reply. "Right. Okay. Well. See you on Monday, Natalie." He turned around hastily and tripped his way down the hall.

The child took pride in watching him go. Though he would never have admitted it, Koda had been giving the male agent an especially hard time. He did not know exactly why.

He just disliked everything about the man. From his stupid beard to his stupid voice to his stupid smile.

Wellington looked down at him with a raised eyebrow.

Koda smirked.

The caseworker rolled her eyes. "You know, not everyone has a master's in psychology." She poked his chest playfully, "Some people might think you're as mean as you act."

"I'm not mean." He poked her back.

"I know that," she replied. "Now, let's get a move on. Before you miss your train and are stuck with me for good!"

Fog had blown in from the lake, outlining everything in ghostly greys. Passersby appeared and disappeared from the mist. Skyscrapers emerged like icebergs. Sounds of trains, cars, and buses echoed off unseen stone. The only visual reminder of the traffic came from yellow lights whisking through the fog. Koda appreciated the gloom. It was comforting, like staying home sick or canceling plans.

In truth, he was more troubled by the people. Men in suits scarfed down lunches while men in hard hats bantered. Some women shopped for their families; others took the day off from theirs. Children did much of everything, especially what they were told not to.

It was as mundane a Monday as had ever been. It felt disrespectful. Insensitive. For though Koda was old enough to know the world would not stop for him, he was young enough to expect it for his father. He held the urn prominently, hoping strangers would see it and offer sympathy.

Not that he wanted any, of course. He just wanted people to know and act accordingly. To hunch over, frown, and shuffle morosely. But as the city went on without regard for him, he went on without regard for it.

It was not hard to do. The city was mostly rows of dull squares, anyway—all painted in either black, white, or—if the builder was feeling creative—beige. The city looked like a giant set of Ikea furniture. Koda put up his hood, kept his head down, and counted the steps it took to cross each section of sidewalk.

Yet, as they neared the station, his gaze wandered across the river. Sitting at an easel was an old man. His racing brush made Koda pause. The boy mumbled, "Why would he paint any of this?"

Agent Wellington looked around. She could have told him that adults pay a hefty sum to tour the riverwalk. She could have said that many artists gladly stayed poor to live downtown, that this was a city people write home about—even if they had never been there. She could have listed all the poems inspired by its parks, the novels written in its cafés, the movies filmed on the lakefront. But Koda would not have cared. So, the caseworker sighed a smile at him. Then, just as she was about to say something nice (and as Koda was getting ready to resent her for it), they heard a horn.

The caseworker glanced behind. "Ah. On time for once!" She clicked her tongue and quickened her pace. "Hurry, Koda. This train must be magic!"

The train smelled like wet laundry. The other passengers looked like wet laundry: unsorted and wrinkled.

"I am getting a snack," Agent Wellington said. "Want anything?"

Koda declined. It made him queasy to think about getting crumbs on his father's urn. His caseworker got up and for a while, the child relaxed. He even picked a particularly stubborn booger that had been annoying him all morning. However, when he went to flick it, he noticed a cross-eyed man looking at him. Koda quickly diverted his attention (and his finger).

Minutes later, he looked at the man again; the fellow was staring right back at him. He had a lumpy gut and the face of a shrew. Not a friendly face. Probably got that gut from drinking. The stranger smiled at Koda. It was the type of smile adults use when they are uncomfortable, more a twitch than a display of kindness. He decided the man must be up to no good and looked for a new seat.

All the other rows were taken, except for one woman with a section to herself. She was middle-aged and seemed preoccupied. "Can I sit with you, miss?"

She seemed to wake from a dream, "Oh. Yes. Of course. But where is your mom?"

"Don't have one."

"Your dad?"

Koda tapped the white box.

"Oh... Poor thing." She patted the seat next to her.

Koda sat and began swaying his feet. He could sense the woman was feeling sorry for him, which unnerved him. He flinched a smile at her.

She frowned; deep smile lines around her eyes kept her looking happy. "Are you all alone, then?"

"Uh uh," he replied. He thought of lying about brothers and sisters he did not have. He had done that before and that always did the job. If he really sold it, he sometimes believed it himself. Though on that day, he was too tired to care.

Agent Wellington returned with a handful of snacks. She panicked when she did not see Koda where she had left him.

Finding him with a stranger, she stormed up with a shrill voice. "Excuse me, ma'am."

Koda blinked. Adults always use 'excuse me' so creatively. "Oh, is he yours?"

The caseworker ignored the question and asked her own, "Why are you sitting over here?"

Koda peeked out from his enclave at the creepy man. "He kept looking at me."

"*He* is just minding his own business," said the agent. "People can be quiet, Koda. It doesn't mean they are bad. It's the loud ones I watch out for."

Koda blurted, "Like my dad?"

His caseworker coughed, "Oh, uh..." She suddenly became very interested in other topics, "What is your name, ma'am?" She sat beside Koda and turned her head so he would not ask her any more questions.

The women began their boring back and forth: ask each other your name; inquire about what you do for a living; ping pong a few customary *Oh's*, *Wow's*, and *Nice's*. Then, plop your face in front of your phone and say not a peep.

Koda rested his hand on his chin and looked out the dusty window. They were zipping across the city. Objects zoomed in and out of view in a blur. Koda imagined the train was a massive paintbrush wet with a thousand colors, now painting the outdoors in a single stroke. This made him sad. He missed his paints. Except for dinosaur figurines, which were unquestionably the coolest toys ever created, his paint set was his favorite possession. But like the rest of his things, those had been in the storage unit his father had forgotten to pay for.

Suddenly, the bottom of the train began to rattle. That caused a few of the passengers to lift their heads from their phones. The middle-aged woman noted, "We're going awfully fast."

Wellington chomped down on a mouth full of snacks, "I'm sure the conductor knows the speed limit."

Koda smooshed his cheek against the window. The train was chugging along next to a river. Ahead, two gates of a railroad crossing were standing upright. Koda thought they looked like royal guards with tall, bayonetted rifles. Yet as he stared at the unflinching gates, he grew uneasy. Those guards never lowered their rifles and headlights kept zooming across the tracks, ignoring the oncoming train.

Koda stared at the river below and asked, "Why isn't the conductor honking his horn?"

Suddenly, a force of impact rippled through the train. Agent Wellington threw a hand over Koda's chest, though that did not prevent him from flying forward. Up became down, down became up again. Luggage spilled out from the overhead storage. The great steel snake groaned and crumpled. Windows shattered and mud slid into the carriage.

Koda clenched his father's ashes as he bounced and tumbled. When water burst through the windows, he held on to the urn as long as he could. But the roaring torrent ripped away his father's remains. "Daddy!" Koda shrieked.

The water was rising. Soon, there would be no way off that train.

VISIONS OF HOME

KODA AWOKE IN FRONT of a splintered door. Torn from its hinges, it was lodged diagonally in the doorway. A small gap, large enough for him to crawl through, occupied Koda's attention. He had seen this door before, as he had the creaky porch, the cracked windows, and the colorless wood. The walls of the house were so pale, they looked sick. The windows were so smudged, they reflected nothing.

Koda pinched his eyes shut. Usually that was enough to wake up, or at the very least change his dream. When he opened his eyes, however, the unhinged door remained. The darksome hole beckoned him to crawl through. He squatted, tilting his head inquisitively. Like a mouse drawn to a crack in the wall, he felt compelled to explore. Curiosity overwhelmed his instincts.

He entered the ruins of his childhood home.

The living room was brighter than the dirty windows had him believe. Koda squinted upwards. Instead of a vaulted ceiling and a brightly lit chandelier, he saw the sun through a hole in the roof. A bird chirped overhead.

Koda wandered through the collapsed room. A chunk of roof had fallen onto the family piano, scattering black and white keys everywhere. The green sectional was so sunken, it looked like it was smirking. Koda thought about sitting down, but the cushions seemed *too* green. Almost fuzzy. He wandered on, hoping to go upstairs and see his bedroom. He got excited. Maybe his toys were up there all along? Maybe his paints and dinosaurs were not in the storage unit? He took a single stride before gulping down his hope. The stairs were blocked by a fat tree root. He could not get past, either by jumping or squeezing, crawling or climbing. Koda stared wistfully up and sighed. It was probably not safe to go up there, anyway.

The only path forward was through the kitchen. Koda tiptoed through the mess. The floor crunched underneath him. Thinking he was stepping on leaves, he glanced at his feet. To his shock, he *was* stepping on leaves. And not just a stray leaf that blows in while the door is open. Oh, no! This was a proper carpet, with a crunchy top layer and a cushiony bottom.

The kitchen was worse off than the living room. Cabinets were bird nests. The dishwasher was a fox den. The refrigerator was a rodent high-rise. And just when he thought the house could not get any more ruinous, he saw the adjacent room.

A huge tree had planted itself in the dead center of the sunroom. Only, to call this a tree was like calling the ocean an aquarium. Technically true, but woefully underselling it. It looked more like a church organ, with wooden pipes branching up and up. There were trunks like columns and limbs like walls. There were boughs like rooves and leaves like shingles. It was not so much a tree as a mossy, pillared hall.

Koda's curiosity again got the better of him. He approached the strange tree and saw a hollow in the central trunk. It was the perfect size for him and would make quite the fort. With a few blankets, it might even be cozy. He climbed into the hollow, stretched out, and suddenly became very tired. For a time, he fought his listless eyelids. Then, he let out a long yawn and plunged into a deep sleep.

SWEETWATER RIVER

WHEN KODA WOKE, HE was not in his woody nook. He coughed up a cloud of dirt and lifted his head. His neck was stiff and his cheeks were indented with a maze of little lines. His knees popped when he got to his feet.

He found himself on the bank of a bubbling brook. A cool mist wafted above the water. Running alongside the stream was a forest alight in fiery, fall colors. Each bough was a burst of light, a sea of dappled sunsets. Koda called out, "Miss Wellington?"

The wind replied with a lonely *whoosh*. Then, silence.

Koda gulped. Nobody was nearby. Certainly not a city full of cars and people. It was getting darker by the minute. The eaves were casting shadows. "I should stay right here," Koda told himself. "Someone will find me."

For a moment, he did just that. Then, he began thinking about all the things that live in the wild. The whishing, whooshing wind made him wonder if there were wolves about. He scanned his surroundings again, hoping to see a search party. Nothing. No one. Hopeless, Koda kicked a rock. "Even if people know where I am, they won't look for me."

Koda glanced at the forest. There were probably nasty bugs in there. He gazed at the water. He would rather not get his shoes wet. He must have turned in all directions a dozen times, each way looking worse than the last. So, he searched for a place to sit. But just then, he saw a shiny object under the trees: a white box with a fern-shaped latch.

He approached the urn. At first, it lay at the forest's edge. Then, Koda got paranoid and looked behind his shoulder. Seeing nothing, he turned back around. Strangely, the urn was no longer as near as it had seemed. It was now a few strides past the eaves, in a clearing. Koda rubbed his eyes which was again a mistake. For when he searched the clearing, he saw the urn was actually well within the darksome forest.

Before long, so was he.

Koda trudged deeper and deeper. Yet with every step, the remains did anything but. They evaded him. Figuring he was imagining things, he paused. This was another dream. The water had snatched the urn. It should not be here without a dent or scrape (and to be fair, neither should he). Still, he could not bring himself to leave the remains, real or not.

Suspecting some sort of trick, he changed his approach. He crouched and crept toward the white box, stalking it like an animal. Slowly, methodically, he closed in on his father. When he blinked, though—the box was more than double the distance away.

Koda slammed his foot down, "Stop moving!"

The box glinted.

Koda gave up on subtly. He bent his knees and broke into a sprint. It was the fastest he had ever run. He darted through the underbrush, kicking up freshly fallen leaves. The forest floor groaned and began to stretch. Though, it was not so much the trees and ground that stretched out as it was the distance between everything. It was like Koda was trapped in a picture that, whenever he took a step, zoomed in a little. What was once a small distance between him and his father was now a great chasm.

It was soon clear the only thing he could catch was his breath. Defeated and sweaty, he blew a gust of air up his brow, pushing his bangs out of his eyes. The leaves he had just kicked up were now far ahead of him, falling onto his father's ashes.

Koda stared at his feet. They pointed away from each other, one toward his father and one back toward the river. He muttered softly, "He is not my responsibility anyway." The words consoled him, so he said them again for good measure. "He is not my responsibility. Not anymore." He turned away from the fern-laced urn.

That caused the forest to shiver. The trunks twisted and the boughs bent, making a straight path back to the river. Koda blinked, confused. He took ten small steps and returned to the water's edge.

His stomach gurgled. The child had not had anything to eat or drink since the morning. He knelt at the stream's edge and cupped his hands. He slurped the cool water and to his shock, it tasted like juice! Koda took a few hearty gulps from the stream. He savored the sweetwater and was soon quite full.

He wiped his mouth and decided the stream did not look too deep. Koda stepped into the water confidently. He promptly plummeted to the bottom. The water was up to his waist and worse, the current was suddenly very fast. Koda tried to keep his footing, but it was too strong. He was being pulled downriver.

"Help!" he called.

Nobody came. The water's sweet taste now soured in Koda's slowly sinking mouth. He searched for something to help him and swam for a fallen log. He wrapped his arms around a branch and cried again for help.

"Oi," said a voice. It seemed to be coming from the log. "Stop that yelling!"

"Who is that?" Koda asked. As nobody was nearby, he asked the fallen log, "Can you talk?"

"Of course I can talk," replied the mouthless wood. "Talking is easy. Listening, though. Only *intelligent* beings do that."

"Please," Koda pleaded. "You have to help me get out of this water!"

"If I could do that," the log quaked, "don't you think I would have walked myself out of my current predicament?"

A fish leaped out of the water and scolded, "Stop that screaming you two! You are going to attract Mahuut."

"I'm going to drown!" Koda screamed.

"Good riddance," grumbled the fish, swimming hastily away.

The fallen log rumbled, "Oh, this is just perfect. We had avoided the Fisher's attention for all this time and now you're going to go and lure—" the log shivered and went silent. Even the core of its wood stopped echoing.

Koda clawed and scraped his way atop the log. "What help you were!" He thwacked the wood and strangely, there was no thumping sound. Panting, he looked around.

Not only had the log gone quiet. The leaves of the trees had stopped swaying in the wind. Motionless in the breeze, it was as if the plants were petrified. The waters too were muffled. The rapids were reduced to a faint *tip, tap* like a leaky faucet. The wild river was a whisper. A fearful whisper.

The only movement for a while came from the fish, all racing downstream. The stagnant water became congested. The shallows clogged. The fish flopped atop one another, trying to move themselves through the jam. When that did not work, they started leaping in every direction, frantically fleeing something upstream. The healthiest fish managed to escape the jam by soaring past, but most stayed stranded in the shallows. Then, the lungfish lunged toward the sandy banks and buried themselves hastily in the mud. Seeing this, other fish began stranding themselves.

Koda had been motionless on his perch, but then a perch flew onto the log and motioned. "Flee!"

Koda had no time to ask questions. A bass barreled past, knocking the perch back into the traffic jam below. Then, a hail of guppies flung themselves up. Koda shielded his face and lost his balance. He grabbed the log tightly and without thinking, crawled as quickly as he could. He made the leap to land, splashing into the mud.

He hiked up the streambank. It was full of choking, flailing fish. He had to help them. He bent down to pick one up. It wiggled away and rasped, "Leave us!"

"Why?" Koda asked. "Why are you doing this?"

"Ma-huut," gasped a rainbow trout.

There was that name again. Before he could ask to whom it belonged, however, he was alerted to the creaking of wood. A long shadow stretched down the stream. A moment later, all commotion in the water quieted. The stranded fish floated onto their sides. Their bodies formed an oval, like they were trapped in an invisible net. A net that slowly pulled them upstream. They disappeared into darkness.

Koda stared, spellbound.

Slowly, a rickety canoe came into view. The prow of the boat was red, rotten, and riddled with mushrooms. A huge fishing pole was fastened into place with iron chains. It was so tall, it caused the canoe to lean forward. The edges of the boat began to bubble.

The river current slowed. The water turned green and started to stink. The trees shivered. The wind let out a sigh and every tree within a mile withered. It was as if fall had happened in a single second. The leaves fell like crimson rain.

Koda watched the lumbering vessel float past. In awe of the giant fishing pole, he wondered, '*What does he hope to catch with that? A whale?*' The question made him quiver.

Nobody was aboard the canoe and yet, when Koda shivered at its passing, the boat groaned. The canoe began to turn itself. From aboard the seemingly empty vessel came the *crick-crack* of footsteps.

"Is someone there?" Koda asked. He immediately knew it was a mistake.

The canoe halted; the river stopped completely. Koda's heart raced. He did not think he could simply run away, so he tried introducing himself. "My name is Koda. What is yours?"

The fishing pole tensed. The line grew taut. It was reeling something in.

Koda felt strangely hungry. His stomach growled again. Despite his fear of the rotting boat, Koda began walking toward it. Yet the longer he looked at the canoe, the more starved he felt. He tried to look away. Something tore into his cheek. He tried to step back; his upper lip lifted toward his nose. The child was hooked on the line!

Panicking, he grabbed the empty air in front of his head and yanked. The ghostly canoe rocked in response. So, Koda yanked again. This time, however, a strong force braced the canoe. The pole was plucked like the string of a guitar. A deep, *dum, da, dum,* echoed. The line began to reel itself in. Koda was pulled face-first into the frothing, oozy water. It was no longer sweet or cool, but steaming and putrid.

As he clawed for the shore, Koda called one last time. "Help!"

Like always, there was nobody around to hear him cry. Nobody was going to save him. As he had lived, so would he—

Suddenly, someone swooped down from the treetops. Swift like the wind, a figure fell onto the canoe. A warrior. He slashed at the massive iron chains with a shining sword. He dodged invisible strikes, parried a nasty blow, and hewed the pole. With a loud clang, the chains snapped and the fishing pole fell into the water.

The flow of the river resumed, pulling the pole—and Koda with it—downstream. "I'm still hooked!" He yelled.

The warrior leaped off the canoe and waded toward Koda. He grabbed the line and said, "Hold still."

Koda shut his eyes and did his best. The pressure on his cheek suddenly lifted. He opened his eyes to see his savior. It was a teenager, a few years older than Koda, with tangled, blonde hair that went just past his shoulders. He removed the hook from Koda's mouth and pulled him ashore.

"What was that?" Koda asked.

"Mahuut. The Headless Fisherman." The boy watched the canoe slowly drift downstream. "An evil spirit that haunts this land."

"But there wasn't anyone on the boat," Koda recalled, perplexed. "At least, I didn't see anyone's face."

The boy took out a canteen. The stream was now clear and shiny. "Evil does not have a face," replied the warrior. He filled the canteen with sweetwater. "Especially in the spirit world."

Now Koda *knew* he was dreaming. He told the figment of his imagination, "There is no such thing as spirits."

The older boy stared at him. He wore no shirt nor shoes and—due to the many holes in his jeans—practically no pants. "If you ask some folks around here, they'll say there's no such thing as humans."

Koda had no reply to that.

"What's your name, kid?"

"Koda. Yours?"

"Koda. That's a nice name. Mine's Teo." That was not his name, in fact. But *'Teo'* was not going to give his true name to some stranger. "You should be more careful out here." He wiped his blade on a pile of fallen leaves.

The sword had looked clean to Koda's eye, but perhaps spirits had invisible blood. If so, Teo could not be a spirit, as he had numerous small cuts on his arms and shoulders. The warrior ignored those and sheathed his sword.

"Where is here?" Koda asked. "I was on a train and it crashed and now... I'm lost."

"Aren't we all?" Teo asked sarcastically.

Koda could not help it. He began to cry. It was the first time in a long while that he had let himself do so. He heard the ghost of his father say, *"Stop that. Nobody cares about a man's tears."* He clenched his jaw, shivered, and hid his face.

"Hey, uh..." Teo coughed uncomfortably. "Don't do that." He shuffled awkwardly, "Look. Why don't you just follow me. I'll, uh. I'll get you on the right path home."

"Really?" Koda asked. He immediately stepped back, "How do I know *you* aren't an evil spirit?"

Teo simply shrugged. "How do any of us know that?" He walked into the forest.

Koda licked the inside of his lips. He did not trust easily, especially where spirits and demons were concerned. He waited on the banks of the stream until the last sliver of sunlight slipped below the horizon. Then, he ran after Teo.

"Just for the night!"

BENEATH THE SPIRIT SKY

THE THICKET SOON THINNED. Koda looked back at the forest. It had seemed so much bigger when he was chasing his father's urn. In reality, it was barely a mile from end to end—just a sparsely wooded section of a vast plain, a vassal of the riverside. Looking at it now, it seemed less like a forest and more like a big spine— like vertebrae of a leviathan swimming through sweeping waves of wheat.

Koda preferred the grassland to the forest. It was less scary in the open. He could see all around him and the grass made less noise when stepped on. He never had to guess that a crunch or crack came from some unseen creature.

Teo felt similarly. Once the forest was out of sight, he stopped and made camp. It did not take long. As they had no tent, they clung to the slopes of a small hill to hide from the wind. And as Teo forbade a fire, they shivered in the dark. Koda tried not to think about how cold he was. Or how sad. He stomped some wheatgrass to make a bed, curled up beneath the heel of the hill, and hoped the wind would die off soon.

For a time, Koda hid within his hoodie. Wrapped like a roly-poly, he did not notice the night sky. Once it petered off, he peeked out from his cocoon. It was brighter than he expected, so he took off his hood and looked up. "Why are there so many stars tonight?"

Teo glanced up. "Same amount as every night. Humans have just gotten used to staring at their own lights."

"I've never seen it so... lit up. Like a Christmas tree!" Koda had thought he knew what the night sky looked like. He had lived in the country, back when his parents were together. He had never seen constellations that changed colors. He had never seen green and blue stars twinkling within a spiraling cosmic fog. It was like he had stumbled upon a galactic dance recital.

"You've never seen the Milky Way before?" Teo asked, half smirking and half frowning.

"I have!" Koda said defensively. "Just... Not like this."

Teo chuckled.

"What's so funny?" Koda glared.

"I'm just messing with you," he grinned. "This is the Spirit Sky. It's not ours." He took a swig from his canteen.

Koda did not like being tricked, especially by other kids. He was about to insult the older boy when Teo asked, "So, how'd you die?"

"I didn't."

"Mm, okay."

"How'd *you* die?" Koda inquired.

Teo squinted at his shoulder, at a mosquito that was taking more than his fair share. He swatted it and shooed, "Get on, you glutton. No double-dipping!"

"Yaaaow!" The mosquito yelped. Its squashed body re-inflated and buzzed off, uttering a few words that are better left unsaid.

Teo then acted as if he had forgotten the conversation, "Damn mosquitos. They love human blood more than anything. Can't get much out here, though."

Koda would not let him off that easily. He asked again, "How did you die?"

The teen was quiet for a time. Though he was barely clothed, he was not shivering. "Do you remember being born?"

Koda shook his head.

"Maybe it's the same for dying."

The older boy was weird. From the little bit of facial hair and the occasional voice crack, Koda guessed he was only a few years older than him. Yet, he sometimes spoke—as he was doing now—in a wise and mournful way. Certainly not the way most teenagers speak.

"Who are you?"

"Teo," he lied.

"I know that, but who? What do you do?"

In no mood to talk, the boy turned. "Get some sleep."

Koda shot him a nasty look and rolled over. He tried to sleep. Though, the quiet of the plains unnerved him. He tossed and turned, craving a siren's reassurances or traffic's lullaby. But there was none of that. Just silence. And the silence was too loud to sleep through. It was unnatural, or rather—too natural. It simply would not do. Koda sat up.

Teo was now perched on the only landmark for miles around: a decaying tree stump. "I don't like the quiet, either." He sighed and leaned back, "Truth is, I don't know what I'm doing out here. Same as you. I feel like I woke up from a long dream."

Koda sat beside him, "Were you on the train, too?"

Teo thought deeply before shaking his head. "The last thing I remember, I was auditioning for a play. But when I got on stage, nobody was there. I went home and my house was in ruins. My brothers, my sisters, my mother. All gone."

Teo stared wide-eyed into the memory. "I didn't think too much of the ruined house. My dad must have had another outburst. I didn't care. I just wanted my dog. But I couldn't find him anywhere. Not in the yard where he'd dig holes. Not on the couch where he'd stink it up with his farts. Not even on my bed. No... Something else was on my bed. Something wild. A tree. Not like any tree I'd ever seen. Sprouted right through my mattress. There was a hollow in the trunk. I went and—"

Koda interrupted excitedly, "I had that dream, too! Well, not the part about the play. Or the sisters. I don't have sisters. Or brothers. Or a dog. My dad wouldn't let me have a dog. But still!"

Teo's blue eyes glimmered in the starlight. He smiled and now, seemed as young as he probably was. He said, voice cracking, "I bet that hollow was a gateway or something. Like a fairy tale! Maybe if we find the tree again, we can both go home!"

Koda's enthusiasm evaporated.

"What's wrong?"

Koda admitted reluctantly, "I don't have a home to go back to."

"Your parents don't have a house?"

"My mom does. But it's not my house."

Teo scoffed, though he did not mean to. He was simply confused. "What do you mean it's not yours? Of course it is. What, you renting? You got foreclosed, huh?"

"No, not that." His mind was racing with lies to tell. He did not have the energy to be honest anymore. Not about this. "It doesn't matter. We're probably dead anyways."

"Well I'm going to find out. And if you want to come with me, you can. You'll have to be a little cheerier than this, though."

Dejection being the mute button of conversation, Koda went quiet. All he could muster were iterations of the same frown.

Annoyed, Teo grumbled, "Look. Mahuut is the master out here. If you want to stay in the spirit world forever, that's your choice." He then made a joke he immediately regretted. "You've got a nice young face. Some fat on you. You'll make for great taxidermy. Mahuut might mount you next to a marlin, if you're lucky."

Koda burst into tears.

There were few things that made Teo uncomfortable: snakes, women, and vulnerability. He chewed on his cheek, waiting for the tears to pass. Yet they never did. Things just got worse and worse. "You don't have anyone in the real world that will miss you?"

Koda immediately thought of his caseworker, Miss Wellington. That only produced more tears, though they were a different kind and more pleasant than the ones prior. They soothed him so that soon, he was wiping his eyes.

Once the crying was just a spatter of sniffles, Teo cleared his throat. "Look. If we're dead, we're dead. If we find the hollow of the tree and it doesn't take us home—fine. So be it. We can throw ourselves off a cliff for fun."

Koda giggled.

Teo smiled. "And if we aren't..." He tapped his legs rhythmically and looked everywhere but at Koda. "You probably have a friend from school you could stay with, right?"

Koda wiped his nose and snorted up his snot. "I move schools too much to make friends."

Teo sighed, "Well now you've got me."

Koda recoiled slightly. "Really?" He blinked a dozen times, half-expecting to wake up from the dream he was obviously in.

Teo scowled at him, "Don't you get mushy on me."

He replied breathily. "I—thank you."

Teo stood up quickly and mimicked Koda's words. "Me—you're welcome." He brushed his legs off, as if sincerity was something to be wiped away. "We should keep going. The Headless Fisherman is never too far away."

Koda followed his lead, dusting himself off. He was still unsure about Teo. But company is the kindling of hope and

Koda was glad to have both. He started going south, "Where do you think the tree is?"

Teo laughed, "Not that way. You'll walk right into Mahuut's Mire."

Koda popped his lips, "Oh, okay." He turned left and lifted one foot.

"I've been that way, too. Just before I found you. Not a pleasant trip." (Indeed it was not, as it led to the Ocean of Unfathomable Agony.)

Teo sipped from his canteen. "See that star," he pointed. "The big, red one?"

"Mhm."

"We follow that. It'll be the only direction I haven't gone yet."

The idea of skipping bedtime and walking around all night was a strange thought. It was something adults did, and not the good kind. "What do we do during the day?"

"Sleep, I guess. Or relax. Like this." Teo offered a sip of sweetwater to Koda, who took it gladly. He expected the same cocktail of juices. Sweet mango, delicious orange, and soothing pineapple. Instead, he got a diluted, bitter mixture. It made him gag. Koda gave the canteen back in a hurry.

"What? You don't like it?"

The child spat. "It tastes worse now."

"Oh, yeah. You get used to that. You just gotta drink a little more than you did last time." He offered the canteen again.

"I'm okay." After that, Koda was sure he never wanted to drink 'sweet' water again.

THE WARNING

THE NIGHTTIME MARCH WAS pleasant. It turns out flat grasslands make for great stargazing. And for not having slept, the boys felt very energized. However, as they walked, Koda began to feel odd. He tried to think of a word that described it. You or I might have proposed *restless*, and while that would be an adequate description—Koda did not think of it. As the sun rose, he finally found the word for it.

"What is it?" Teo inquired.

"It's like I am a zombie. We've been walking for hours and my feet don't hurt. I'm not tired at all."

Teo grinned, "You're in the spirit world. How much rest do you need?"

"True," Koda admitted. He bolted down the rivets in his shaking voice and asked as if he did not care about the answer, "I'm not a zombie, am I?"

"No. You don't smell bad enough."

Koda smirked, "You do."

The shirtless teen turned and parted the greasy hair from his eyes. He sniffed, "Hmm. What is that? Is that... Brains?!" He sprinted toward Koda.

The younger boy fled up a hill, giggling all the while until the teenager grabbed him. Laughing, Koda pleaded for mercy.

Teo hissed at him, lunged for a bite, and then stopped. Something caught his eye, and the play ended. He gestured east, "Sun's rising."

"Should we stop?" Koda asked.

"Nah," said Teo. "Not yet. But we shouldn't run off like that. Once the red star is gone, we'll be travelling blind."

They continued for a while in the light, doing their best to go straight. Although they did not get tired, they still got just as bored. No matter how long or far they walked, nothing changed around them. During the day, the plains just went on and on. Just brown, brown, and would you have guessed it—more brown. It was like a gigantic, grassy treadmill. Irritated by their lack of progress, Koda kicked the dirt in frustration.

"Hey!" the dirt yelled back. "Watch where you swing that stomper!"

If Koda had jumped any more, his spine would have sling-shotted out of his body. "The dirt, it's talking!"

Teo rolled his eyes and told him to apologize, then.

Koda gulped, "I, uh. I'm sorry for kicking you, Dirt."

The ground began to bubble and turn itself over. Then, a little prairie dog burrowed upward. It shook the stray silt off its brow and glared at the boys. "Are you really that dense? A bit of stray sandstone in your noggin?"

Koda thought of the talking log and scratched his head. "I just thought, given this is the uh, uh—"

The prairie dog climbed out of his hole. "Yes, yes," he scolded them. "The spirit world. Where rodents finish more sentences than humans. Get used to it."

Teo stepped in front of Koda, "Look. He's sorry for kicking you."

"He did not *kick* me. You two are stomping all over my roof!"

"Then he's sorry for that, too. Look, we're not here to stomp on your home." He explained they were looking for a tree.

This, as you might have guessed, caused the prairie dog to chuckle. "Not many of those out here."

"It's probably a big tree," Koda added.

"Is it now? I would have guessed it'd be awfully small, as trees tend to be."

Koda tried to explain but he was no arborist. "It has lots of big trunks. It's like a forest, but it's one tree."

That changed the animal's demeanor. The prairie dog crouched, looked around suspiciously, and whispered, "The Banyan?"

"You know it?" The boys asked in unison.

"I *knew* it," answered the critter. "It's been a long while since I ventured that far. Especially above ground. It is not a happy place."

"We have to go there," Teo explained.

"Why in all the grassland would you want to do that?"

Teo did not answer. "You know where it is, then?"

Barking a laugh, the animal answered, "Of course. It's kind of hard to miss." He pointed in the direction they were already going, at a cobblestone path barely visible in the grass. "Do us all a favor and follow the road."

Teo did not have the best of manners. Seeing the path, he quickly ended the conversation. "Awesome. Cool. See ya." He jogged away (causing dust to rain from the rafters of the prairie dog lodge).

The animal scowled and muttered about 'proper etiquette.'

"Sorry about him," Koda knelt. "He says things in funny ways sometimes. Like 'thank you.' What is your name, by the way?"

The animal squinted at him. "Names are powerful. You first."

The child did not hesitate. "Koda."

"Koda," the animal repeated. "You wouldn't happen to be a medicine man?"

The boy shook his head.

"A pity. I always liked them." He stared at the boy curiously for a while until Koda pressed him for his name. He frowned slightly and said, "To you, I will be François."

"Just to me?" Koda inquired.

The prairie dog nodded. "My original name was given long ago, before there were languages to speak it. Besides, humans have such short memories. François should be challenging enough to remember."

"Well," Koda said, trying his hardest to not seem confused (and offended). "Thank you, François."

The animal stared at Teo, stomping through the prairie. "*You* are welcome." At that, the exchange was at an end. Or it should have been. But then, the prairie dog said something altogether odd. "Do you know the meaning of your name?"

"What? Uh, no."

"Hm. I thought not." The animal eyed the sky nostalgically. "Many old wanderers had your name. The medicine men of old. To them, it meant *friend*."

"I don't have many of those," Koda admitted.

"I daresay that will change," François stated.

"Really?" the child asked excitedly. He whispered, "Do you predict the future?"

The question was so heartwarmingly naïve, the prairie dog was taken aback. Perhaps he had misjudged this wanderer. "I do not. At least, not intentionally. However—" His conscience swelled to the forefront. He curled his claws, beckoning Koda to come closer. "I will say this: The road that will take you to the Banyan is not a safe one."

"Is it the only way?" Koda asked.

"For your kind, yes," François answered. "I do not envy you. Or your friend, especially. And I don't like him at all.

But you, you have a proper way about you, young wanderer. So, if you see a cabin on the path, stay away. I should hate for the owner of that cabin to get *you*."

"Who lives there?"

"Not *who*, but *what*."

That was the last the boys saw of the prairie dogs, at least for a while. Yet, it was not the last the dogs saw of them. They made sure the boys had left their lands for good. Then, after they had passed, the entire lodge was boarded up, the trapdoors were reinforced, and a watch was set around the prairie. Bad things came from the Banyan in those days.

The boys soon came upon a cobbled road that meandered into a shallow gully. The rounded rocks in the ravine echoed, causing their quiet footfalls to clang among the claystone crags. Beside them were the bent remains of rusted lampposts, now blotched green with lichen. The change of scenery was at first welcomed. Then, dusk came with many clouds and the lampposts did not turn on.

Koda called for a rest. Not to sleep, mind you—he just did not like the shadows leaning into the gully. Teo would have preferred to keep trekking, but he gave in when he realized he had not had any sweetwater that day.

They found a sandy patch to lie on. Koda looked up at the clouds, Teo drank from his canteen, and both expected to hear silence. Instead, a patch of pebbles peppered a nearby slope. Koda sat up just in time to see a cloud of dust settle. Teo muttered disinterestedly, "Rabbit."

Koda was not sure. He held his breath and stared. For a minute or more, all was still and silent. Then, he heard the slightest shifting of fabric from behind two boulders.

Teo sat up. A few more seconds went by. Whatever had made the dust cloud was *trying* to stay quiet. Not one peep came, no pebble strayed. Yet, the setting sun had not disappeared entirely. The sneaker's shadow peeked out from behind the boulders, betraying its host.

Koda pointed at the twig of swaying darkness.

Teo nodded and unsheathed his sword. "Who is there?" he demanded.

Something scuttled behind the stones. The shadow flickered.

"Who are you?" Teo asked, deepening his voice.

"Maybe we should keep going," Koda whispered. The memory of Mahuut's hook was still on his lip.

"I don't run from anything," declared the proud teenager. "Show yourself, spirit!" When no reply came, he leapt atop the boulder.

Suddenly, a figure in a black hood and cloak flew backward. With a shriek, it fled deeper into the gully.

"Oh no you don't," Teo growled. He jumped down and took chase. Koda yelled for him to stop, but Teo would not listen. "It'll only come back. That's what evil spirits do if you don't confront them."

That was correct, of course. Though, evil spirits rarely let themselves get caught and usually do the catching. So, as Koda raced up the slope, he feared this was all a trap. He suspected something even before he reached the top of the ravine. Then, when he did reach the top—he quivered. For he saw what the prairie dog had warned him about: the cabin.

The structure was old. The roof was slouching, the chimney was crooked, and the rotting, wooden walls were warped. Everything was out of place, giving the cabin a sinister look—like it was snarling at you.

Koda would have fled right then and there. He would have said, "Nope," and turned right around, not looking back for many miles. And years after, he would deny he had seen it at all. He would have done this, had Teo not marched right up to the haunted cabin and knocked on the door with the hilt of his sword.

Koda hissed, "We shouldn't be here."

"We have to confront it," Teo said stoically. "Or else it will keep following us." Neither could have known that worse spirits were stalking them even now.

Koda crept up the patio steps. Like trumpets, they creaked. "The prairie dog warned us to avoid this place."

"He didn't warn me," Teo muttered. He put a hand on Koda's shoulder. "Look, kid. If you run from things out here—it's only a matter of time before they get you. Trust me."

Suddenly, footsteps skittered from behind the cabin door.

Teo tightened his grip on his sword and thwacked the door twice. "Open up, spirit! There are some manners that need teaching." After waiting several seconds, Teo took a deep breath, put a hand on the doorknob, and twisted.

Koda held his breath.

Just then, the door burst open, knocking the older boy onto his back. His sword fell ringing and he lay unconscious. Koda rushed to Teo's side. He tugged his arms and tried pulling him up. But then, the floorboards groaned and Koda froze. Trembling, he looked up. A pale figure stared down at him.

THE HERMIT

"Oh dear," said a soft-spoken old man. He raised his bushy brow, "I'm afraid that will leave a mark." He glanced backward, "Yuck. This place is a mess. No helping that now I suppose." He smiled so awkwardly at Koda, rust may have flaked off his cheeks.

The fellow looked more like his grandpa than a ghoul or ghost. He wore a white collared shirt tucked into wrinkled, red corduroy pants. Over his shirt was a grey vest with accessories stuffed in the pockets. Bifocals were clipped to a lanyard on his chest pocket. These he put on before saying, "W-would you help me bring your friend inside?"

Koda nodded confusedly. He grabbed Teo's legs and helped carry him into the cabin. They laid him gently on a green, feathery bed. The old man scurried to a wood fireplace and threw a log into the fire (never mind the fact it was a hot summer evening). A tea kettle hung from a metal rack over the fireplace.

The cabin was a single, rustic room. Nailed over the doorway were two goat's hooves. They were angled toward the ceiling and held a rifle. To the right was the bed Teo slumbered in. It was a cushioned twin-sized with a canopy. To the left was a table with dust on all but the biggest chair. Scattered on the table were knickknacks, papers, and paints.

Koda drifted unconsciously toward the table. A half dozen canvases were strewn across it. Each one was a variation of a single image: a lone flower bulb sprouting in a churning sea. It had yet to blossom and was unpainted.

The old man traced Koda's stare to the table and gasped, "Forgive the mess! And my intrusions. I do not get many visitors."

Koda tore his attention from the paintings. He remembered the prairie dog's warning. "Why were you following us?"

"Well, you see," the man began to pace. "I saw you two from up here and went down to say hello. Though, I'm not a word person. I am bad at hellos and goodbyes, especially. So, when I got to the river bottom, I froze up and did not know how to introduce myself."

"Hello?" Koda suggested.

"Ah," the Hermit frowned. "I wish it were that simple. But I am old and have been alone for a very long time. I did not want to risk scaring you off."

"You did a bad job of that," Teo groaned.

"Yes, I believe I did." The Hermit went to shake the grumpy boy's hand. "Nice to meet you. My name is..." He bit his lip and grew quite confused.

"Yes," asked Teo, sitting up. "Your name is?"

"Nobody has called me by one in so long, I must have forgotten it." The strange man flattened the creases on his vest. "Never mind that. The kettle is boiling and I've not forgotten how to make tea! What are your names?"

As Teo was not going to give some stranger his name, even a fake one, Koda introduced them both.

The Hermit repeated for memory's sake, "Teo. Koda. Got it."

"I don't want any tea," the teenager muttered, crossing his arms.

The Hermit reached into another of his vest pockets and took out something resembling a box of crayons. He flicked open the top. The crayons were all white. "Cigarette, then?"

Teo squinted, arm beginning to rise. He may have agreed if the Hermit had not immediately put them away. "I apologize. That was rather antiquated of me." He gathered plates, cups, and spoons from the cabinet and set them delicately. He then took some old pieces of paper off the floor and folded them into napkins.

Koda and Teo flashed confused looks.

The Hermit saw them and hastily stated, "You must think I'm barbaric." He hunched over his teapot and put in a spoonful of tea leaves.

Koda blinked. "I wouldn't say *that*, exactly."

"Of course not. You seem too polite to say the truth. Nonetheless, I don't blame you if you don't want tea. What kind of host measures with a soup spoon!"

"Yeah," Teo grumbled. "That's it."

The Hermit sighed, "I figured as much. I'm afraid I've lost most of my cutlery over these many years." He carried the teapot to the table, "Oh, enough '*woe is me.*' Come. Sit. Let me make up for my poor introduction."

Koda shrugged, thinking the man was not all that bad (and if he was, it was best not to be rude). Teo scolded him for that, sitting up and murmuring, "He just hit me!"

"On accident," the Hermit insisted. "I promise I was just trying to tidy up a smidge before you two came knocking."

The boys held a brief council near the exit, where Teo argued they should not trust anyone. In the older boy's eyes, everyone was a villain—even if they did not intend to be. At that, Koda shook his head. "He doesn't seem like an evil spirit to me. Just lost."

The Hermit overheard that. "Lost? Yes, aren't we all."

Teo would not budge and took to leaning near the door. He began thinking of gloating things to say when Koda wound up poisoned.

Meanwhile, teatime proceeded without much talking (or drinking, for that matter). The Hermit had gotten his wish,

Koda was sitting with him, and now he was completely unable to speak. He tried, of course. Every time he found something to say, he looked at his feet and muttered to himself.

Koda broke the silence, "So, are you a painter?"

The old man picked up one of the paintings, though it was only a sketch. "I'm not sure anymore."

"What do you mean?" Intrigued, Koda grabbed one of the more finished pieces. "Aside from this flower, this looks really well done."

The Hermit smiled, though he did not seem happy. "I appreciate that. I kept telling myself to finish the painting, to just settle on a color. And yet, every time I thought I had it—I just started over. Now I fear I will never finish it."

Koda grabbed a tube of paint, "What about this green here? For the stem." When the man did not reply, Koda took the initiative and opened the tube. Only, it would not budge. It remained stubbornly shut.

"You see now my dilemma. These paints were gifted to me by a very special woman. I hesitate to call them magical, because that cheapens their charm. But there is a spell to them. They will not open in troubled waters, so to speak."

Teo rolled his eyes. "So to speak. How about not speaking in riddles?"

"Yes, that was rather cryptic. Forgive me. It's just that the truth of things is rather silly. Rather... Embarrassing. You see, one can only use these paints if one is content. Comfortable. Happy."

Koda gazed at the many unfinished paintings. With every iteration, the flower shrunk and the storming sea swelled. From left to right, the colors dwindled until the one held by the Hermit—the final iteration—was just a black and white outline. Koda could not help it; he felt sorry for the old man.

"That's ridiculous," Teo snorted. "What kind of spell does that?"

"One that condones only the creation of goodness and beauty." The hermit set down the sketch and wiped his tired eyes. "One that has grown weary of my cataracted sight."

At that, Teo tried to get Koda's attention. After all, the old man had just said he was neither good nor beautiful. In Teo's mind, that meant he was evil and ugly. The older boy cleared his throat and gestured at the door.

Koda ignored him and changed the subject. "We are looking for the Banyan Tree. Do you know where it is?"

The man's eyes swiveled as he searched his memories. "Hmm. Yes. I think I might have that locked away somewhere." He smiled, "Maybe I will remember more if we keep talking."

That irritated Teo. "We aren't here to be your friends. We have friends. Why are you alone out here, anyway?"

The Hermit struggled to remember that, too. He eventually settled on an answer even he found unsatisfactory. "I wanted to get away from it all. I guess I did too good of a job."

Koda stared at the frowning Hermit, whose life seemed to have left his pale, shriveled skin. Only through his eyes did any youth shine, and those were bright and kind. Koda did not think anyone bad lived behind those homely, blue beacons. "Why were you so afraid of us?"

"The same reason you were afraid of me," he smiled. "I think we all get so lost in our heads, we see people as if they are wearing masks. Masks our eyes put on them."

Teo scoffed, "You were wearing a black cape and a hood."

The Hermit got up and went to his coat rack. Teo stepped warily aside as the old man reached for several garments. Yet he did not take anything from the coat rack. Instead, he bent down and lifted a dark blanket. "I thought you would be cold." He sighed and slumped back in his seat. He sipped his tea and told Teo, "When we are consumed by our demons, we see demons everywhere. What are yours, I wonder?"

The boy glared at him.

The old man coughed. "Beg your pardon." He tried pouring Teo a fresh cup of tea, but his elbow hit the table and he spilled it. "Oh, drat. I've spoiled everything. You must think I am just some blabbering fool."

"No," Koda quickly insisted, fetching some towels. He helped the Hermit soak up the spill, saying, "You just seem scared."

"And out of practice," Teo mumbled.

The Hermit rubbed the back of his head, "Right on both counts, I'd say."

Once the cleaning concluded and they returned to their seats, Koda suggested, "Maybe you should go to a city? Do they have cities in the spirit world? It might help if you just talked to people."

"Hmm," the Hermit rubbed his chin. "You may be right. Though the only city is the Banyan Tree and—" he suddenly cheered. "Hah! There you are, you old sneak. Dust all over you, but I've got ya!" He pulled his hair and peered at his empty hands, "Look here, a stealthy little memory!"

Koda blinked, completely lost.

Teo, however, knew what the Hermit was getting at. "You know where the tree is, don't you?"

The Hermit stood up and walked toward the window. "I do, as I once lived there as a young man. Let me see if I can recall my route and reverse it for you."

He looked down the cliff at the dry river bottom. "Follow the gully... Follow the gully... Hm... Until you get to a meadow! You will find hills that are not hills." He turned and eyed them, "That is the most dangerous part of the journey. They call it—Oh heckerum, what do they call it? Timber—Timberfall, no, not quite. Timbergrave! Yes, that's right. They call it Timbergrave. And it is always watched. If you are seen, vengeful demons will—"

"Oh, what am I saying? You cannot go that way! It is too dangerous!"

Teo snorted, "If *you* could make it through okay, I think *we* will be just fine."

Koda wished Teo would not be so mean. He added, "If that is the way to the Banyan, we have to try."

"It is the only way," said the old man grimly. "But the Banyan is not worth the risk, not anymore. Stay here!"

For a moment, Koda was tempted. Something about the old man just seemed right. The child looked at Teo, who gave him a reprimanding head shake. Frowning, Koda pushed his tea toward his host, "We don't belong here. The spirit world, I mean."

The Hermit stared at the ceiling. "I thought that, too. You get used to infinity."

Teo groaned, "You don't get it. We both saw a vision of the tree. It could be the only way home."

"A vision only means what you want it to mean. How do you know that your *visions* won't lead to your doom?"

Teo turned and put a hand on the doorknob, "Come on, Koda. We have what we need. Let's go."

The Hermit darted to his feet, "The Banyan is no home anymore. It is a prison! A mansion for Mahuut!"

The more terrified the old man became, the more Koda began to agree with him. Besides, he made sense. Why run from a monster right into its lair? He rubbed his lip and thought, *'Maybe there are two banyan trees?'*

The Hermit collapsed in his chair. His shoulders slumped. He twirled a spoon around his cup. He stared thoughtfully at the lukewarm liquid. He sighed and admitted, "I'm not the best person to give traveling advice. I can barely go past my porch."

He eyed Teo and Koda. "You two will go no matter what I say. Isn't that right?"

The boys nodded.

"No matter how sickly the Banyan has become?"

Again, the boys nodded, though Koda did so reluctantly.

"Well," the Hermit took a deep breath, "I would be a bad host not to send you with provisions." He collected various items and placed them in a duffel bag. It was a long and narrow tube of heavy cloth, like the kind Koda's father used to lug around when they were in between places to live. The Hermit placed raincoats, boots, and umbrellas into the bag. "These should keep you dry in Timbergrave. From there, you'll only need to keep an eye on the horizon. The Banyan will be hard to miss."

He hoisted the duffel bag but just then, paused and looked out his window. He nodded to himself after a time and went to the dining table. With his back to the boys, he covertly slipped a few extra items into the duffel bag. Koda did not notice, but Teo did. He squinted at the bag suspiciously. "Very generous of you, sir."

The Hermit peered at the older boy, "You're awfully mature for your age, you know that?"

"We're spirits," Teo replied. "Who knows how old we all are?"

The Hermit popped up his salt and pepper brows; they seemed to lighten to a strawberry blonde. His wrinkles smoothed over and his eyes—they became like mirrors.

Koda took the duffel bag. "Thank you, mister. And I think you *can* go past your porch. You did today, after all."

The Hermit beamed at him with those ever-youthful eyes. "I suppose that's true, isn't it?" He opened the door and took another deep breath. "Perhaps I shall escort you? At least through the gully. Would that be okay?"

The boys spoke at the same time. Teo said no. Koda said yes, and he was louder.

WANDERERS

WHILE THREE MAY HAVE made for a company in the real world, in the spirit world—it made for arguments. Teo begrudged the old man for coming and took every chance to riddle him with questions. With each one, he acted as if he was uncovering a plot. Presently (and despite the fact it was still nighttime), Teo was squinting at the old man's vest. "Why do you wear fancy clothes if you're all alone?"

The Hermit replied, "That is precisely *why* I wear nice things. Clothing reflects the mind state of the individual."

Koda looked down at his baggy hoodie thoughtfully. Meanwhile, the old stoic eyed Teo's bare chest and frayed pants. He tutted his tongue. "I once lived in a tree and I never looked as wild as you."

Teo licked his lips, as he did when the Hermit got the best of him in an argument. He gestured at one of the mossy lampposts. "Did you put these here?"

The Hermit laughed. "Did you see the state of my cabin, dear boy? No, these were here when I arrived. Built long ago by some greater being." As they passed the darkened lamp, he paused and looked up. "One whose power is greatly diminished."

"Have they ever worked?" Koda asked.

"When Ancients walked this world, yes."

Teo was still hoping to catch the man in a lie. "You talk like you've been here a long time. How long have you been dead?"

"How ever should I know?" The Hermit questioned, and he meant it. When the boys did not answer, he shook his head. "That's the tricky thing, I've learned. This is a place for the dead, to be sure, but it is ultimately the realm of the spirit. The Spirit, I should say—with all the formality of a capital."

Koda looked wide-eyed at the man, hanging on his every word. This annoyed Teo more than anything and it caused his voice to twist angrily. "What does that even mean?"

"There is a life force that permeates this world. Long ago, when I remembered my name, the force took the shape of great Ancients. They walked this land as its keepers and—when some wanderer came from the outer lands—they judged them. The worthy ones were admitted to become students, revelers, and worshippers. Some would linger overlong and become Ancients themselves. Most went back to the outer lands—to your world I assume—becoming rulers and wisefolk."

He saw Teo's questioning gaze and continued. "As for the unworthy. Well, they were not much of a problem. They always seemed to go insane." He remarked, "I don't think there's been a worthy wanderer, let alone two, in many an age."

Koda whispered, "We are wanderers?"

"You certainly are. As for me, I'm certain of only one thing." The old man took a deep breath and stared happily at the stars. "I've missed going on walks."

"Maybe *you* are an Ancient?" Koda suggested.

He laughed at the idea, but not in a mean or mocking way. He genuinely thought the boy was joking. When he realized he was not, he quickly apologized. "No, my boy. I may not remember my name, but I remember the Ancients.

I remember how they walked across this vast realm, growing it into a magical place. I remember how they tended to the Banyan, and how wherever they went—beauty followed."

"Where are they now?" Koda asked, though he suspected he knew the answer.

"Dead," Teo guessed. He looked at the Hermit for confirmation.

"Yes," replied the man, whose voice creaked with elderly vibrato. "One of the wanderers that came to this land was Mahuut. He tricked the Ancients into thinking he had a druid's heart and a shaman's mind. In the end..." He trailed off.

"In the end?" Teo repeated, now hooked on the story.

The Hermit shivered. "We should not talk about the Fisherman until the sun is high in the sky."

The boys both pestered him to continue, but the old man refused. And though they begrudged his silence, they would have thanked him had they seen what stalked them now. Lights came from behind, and not from any lamps.

The next day, they passed the last of the strange lampposts. The rock walls of the gully widened. They had come to the mouth of the dry riverbed. Boulders, toppled trees, and other debris spilled out like spittle onto the plain. They wandered through the expanse, clinging to the ever-shortening ridges to stay out of the wind. That lasted only a few minutes before the red rock dove back into the earth, leaving them in an exposed and chilly meadow.

Koda had hoped that would brighten things. The shadows had been terrible in the gully. But even in the open, with the sun high above them, the sky was tinted and the shadows remained. You might have assumed it was a cloudy day, and indeed, that is what Koda thought. There were even polka dots of darkness floating lazily across the flowing hills. So, when he looked up and saw no clouds in the sky, you can imagine his surprise! Koda looked at the old man, questioningly.

"The Penumbra," the elder explained. "It cloaks all of Timbergrave."

Koda pointed at the shady circles dotting the hills, "Where are those coming from?"

"Openings in a ghostly canopy. Rather than letting in light—the dead trees let only darkness through." He pointed, "See those mushrooms growing in the shadows?"

"Mushrooms!" Koda exclaimed. "I thought those were flowers."

"They are the flowers of the dead. You see those, you'll see ghosts soon after."

Teo was skeptical. "I don't see anyone."

The Hermit peered at the gloomy sky. "They see you."

"Who?" Koda questioned nervously.

The old man answered, "The Watchers of this hallowed place, the long-dead Ancients." He shuddered, "I have gone as far as I can."

"What?" Koda whirled around. "After all that, you're going to leave us?"

"This is a sacred place. The Ancients will dislike us all, but they will hate me especially."

"Why?"

"I do not know. Trees have long memories, and I've lived a long life. Perhaps it was because I came from the city, but the last time I was here, an awful storm was summoned to punish me."

"Well, alright then," Teo said. "Can't have that." He was quite ready to be rid of the stranger.

"Fine," Koda grunted angrily. He was a poor liar where his feelings were concerned, and he was often concerned with his feelings. On this occasion, he wished he never had tea with such a kind, cowardly man. "We weren't friends anyway." By his tone, the Hermit knew they had been.

"Dear Koda," the old man began, "I have learned in my life that it is best to end a good thing early, that way it cannot become bad."

"Sounds smart to me," Teo nodded.

"You are both stupid," Koda told them.

The Hermit got on a knee, "I would rather us part as friends than let time make us into acquaintances."

"A valuable lesson," Teo chimed.

"I don't need a lesson," Koda argued defiantly. "You two do. You don't just walk away from your friends."

The Hermit stood up and said with a sad smile, "When you get to my age, my boy, I hope you still feel that way." And so he left, his hair growing a shade whiter. When he got back to his cabin, he immediately felt guilty. For he had left the boys to the demons he could not face. They walked now into that terrible storm. And he had lied about who would create it.

THE PENUMBRA

THE BOYS WERE QUIET for the rest of the morning. As far as Koda was concerned, the Hermit had given up and Teo had let him. By the afternoon, the young swordsman was fed up with the silence. "You can't get attached to people, kid."

"I didn't get attached," Koda corrected. "He was being stupid, that's all."

Teo wiped his blade with a polish. He winked at his reflection and took a swig of sweetwater. He recoiled from the bad taste and took another. "Everyone's stupid. Can't get your hopes up or you'll get hurt."

"Now you sound like him," glared the younger boy.

Teo rolled his eyes, sheathed his sword, and sifted through the duffel bag. "Just a bunch of junk and jackets. A map would have been better." He zipped up the bag and tossed it to Koda, "Of course you liked him."

As the Hermit had been a disappointment, Koda argued. "No I didn't."

Since meeting the old man, Teo's eyes had been pinched narrowly at the sides in a permanent scowl. "Sure you did. You would have stayed with him if I hadn't been there. With a stranger."

"You were a stranger," Koda reminded.

"And I could have been a monster. Look. It's fine. You just trust too easy."

"And you make up your mind too quickly."

"Hey, you put two and two together long enough, you don't need a calculator. I know how his type adds up. But you're just a kid. You haven't had to learn the hard lessons yet."

Koda's face was painted red with frustration. "Stop calling me a kid! You're not much older than I am. And my life wasn't perfect!"

"Oh yeah?" Teo rolled up his sleeves and pointed at a slew of discolored scars. There were at least a dozen slashes, gashes, and bashes. He stared, eyes watery and fiery at the same time. "This one came from a screwdriver. My old man is a whiz with that. This one was from a knife. He says that was an accident. What do you think? And this one—oh, are you squeamish? I'm sorry. I thought we were showing our scars. Where are yours?"

Teo's wounds cut into Koda like aftershocks of an earthquake. He gulped and his voice cracked, "I don't have any."

The pins holding Teo's eyes must have popped out because they widened. His cheeks softened. "Course you do." He sighed and looked to his side. He carried on the conversation as if he were talking to the grass. "Look. We don't need anyone's help. We can get to the Banyan on our own." He glanced at the duffel bag. "That'll just slow us down."

Koda looked at the bag, unsure.

Teo shrugged, "If you think a grown-up can look after you better than you can, that can be your burden."

A few days ago, Koda may have dropped the duffel bag and fended for himself. But a lot can happen in a few days—sometimes years! So, with a deep breath, Koda decided to take his chances. He hoisted the bag over his shoulder.

The Penumbra was calm. Had the Hermit not told them about the ghostly canopy, the boys would never have noticed it. You had to turn your head in just the right way to see it. Yet, if you did manage to catch a glimpse, you would see a gossamer outline of silver branches. An ethereal web woven high throughout the sky, with rays of shadow shooting through the openings. It was like a crumbling roof held up by pillars of darkness.

Beneath the canopy, a warm wind flowed. When the great gust breathed in and out, tall mushrooms stretched and bowed. So many moved in unison, turning and showing their white undersides, that when the wind blew, it looked like an invisible paintbrush moving across the land. All was pleasant for a time. Even Teo relaxed and began to hum (though he had terrible pitch).

Despite the tranquility of the mushroom meadows, Koda began to worry. True clouds—not just ghostly shadows—were forming on the horizon. Storm clouds. They started as loiterers, leaning lazily against the sky. A few grouped together as a grey gang. Then, more clouds joined, jostling with the sky for real estate. Once there was no blue left, they changed color to a rotten rust.

Koda stopped and rummaged through the duffel bag. He pulled out a raincoat and in doing so, revealed something else. A small, wooden handle. For a second, Koda simply stared. Then, he sifted through the bag. He first found seven paint brushes of various sizes, then five of the magic paints. White, black, yellow, red, and blue. He dug to the bottom of the bag, hoping for a blank canvas. The old man had not given him one; he would have to find that himself.

Teo joked, "Gonna paint the sky blue?"

"Maybe," Koda replied. The prospect of having paints, even ones he could not open—energized him. He slipped on a raincoat and smiled in spite of the coming storm.

He offered a raincoat to Teo, but the older boy refused. If he noticed the stench in the air, he did not show it. He did not even sneeze when sooty, sizzling flakes began to fall. Nor did he seem to get itchy when they hit his skin.

Finally, a crackle came from the coppery clouds. Koda scratched his exposed hands, "You sure you don't want a raincoat?"

"It's probably bewitched."

That might have been true. For when the stinking shower started, Koda's skin was protected. The same was not true for Teo, whose body began to blister. The older boy itched his arms furiously and charged deeper into the eye of the storm.

"Just put one on!"

"I don't need anyone's help," Teo growled. He took out his canteen and dumped sweetwater on his wounds. They sizzled and smoked. He gnashed his teeth and bit his lip, "See? All better. This way!"

Koda hesitated. This was no normal storm. Their surroundings darkened as they went. Each breath became harder to take than the last. It felt like the entire cloud had collapsed onto them and they were slowly being swallowed. He tried to keep pace with Teo, but it was like moving through tar. Soon, they were separated. Without the swordsman, Koda quickly lost his way. He looked up and around, hopelessly searching for some way out of the storm. The wind battered him with acid droplets and ripped off his hood, forcing him to stare into the smog.

Smoking silhouettes stared back. Some wore foggy cowls and wielded wispy weapons. Others notched bows from toxic towers. Then, two plumes came together. They wove a complex design until at last—Koda saw it.

The canoe.

Koda sank to his knees as the massive boat grew and grew. The great fishing pole had been repaired and two, giant hands now held it in place. The foggy silhouettes began to chant. Hunting horns sounded and slowly, the fishing pole craned back. The Headless Fisherman cast his line.

At last, Teo reappeared. He leaped in front of Mahuut's hook and knocked it away with his sword. He turned to Koda, "This way! Follow me!"

The child would have liked to, yet his legs had turned to stone. Try as he might to lift them, he was too scared to move. He looked up at Teo's sooty, scarred face and shook his head.

"You're not allowed to give up," Teo growled. With one hand he parried the fisherman's hook, with the other he dragged Koda to his feet. "Come on, kid. Be brave!"

A teenager had not said those last words. They resonated with years of wisdom and empathy. They were not the cold or callous quips of a scarred child. Those words belonged to someone else. Yet, it was Teo who had said them. Such strength did they carry that they lifted Koda's legs and kept him upright as he ran.

Teo led him to a cliff face carved flatly into the side of a hill. At its foot was a circular door. Teo heaved it open, "In here!"

Koda feared what might be in there, in the forgotten underground. But he feared what was outside more. Left with little choice, they charged into the unknown.

TIMBERGRAVE

THE FIRST THING THE boys noticed about their new surroundings was the smell. The space was no nose-wrinkler, to be sure—but it was no sweetly scented candle, either. In a word, it smelled old. Kind of like how your grandmother's house might smell, with scents and odors that modern times do not make anymore.

They were in a chamber with tall, vaulted ceilings. The room looked like it had been whittled out of a single block, without the use of nails or screws. Teo put a hand on one of the walls. A thick layer of dust came off. He brushed off more of the dust, reaching as high as he could. From what they could see, thin sections of wood had been laid one after another from the bottom of the room to the very top.

"Like growth rings on a tree," Teo said to himself. He walked toward a darkened room.

Koda dared not speak until he was sure Mahuut was not coming in after them. He watched as the reckless boy walked calmly toward the darkness. He glared as the swordsman casually remarked on the craftsmanship of the cave. Finally, when the thunder abated and the rain stopped tap-dancing on the roof, Koda yelled, "You almost got us killed!"

Teo raised his brow, "You almost got yourself killed." He lifted his hand and wiggled two fingers, "Legs. You still have them, right?"

Koda *was* embarrassed about that. He should have run. Rather than admit it, he did what any self-respecting arguer would do. He deflected, "You should have put on the Hermit's raincoat!"

"I don't trust people who haven't earned it."

Koda groaned and went to leave.

"Woah," yelled Teo. "Hold on, kid. Don't you want to explore?"

"No," said Koda firmly. "The old man said this place was haunted."

"Yeah," Teo agreed. "By Mahuut. Come on, kid. Be brave. Besides, he said *Timbergrave* was haunted. We don't know what this place is. It could be a shortcut that takes us *around* Timbergrave."

Koda thought about it for a moment. Although he would have preferred to be right, he had to admit that made sense. He mumbled as much to Teo, who instantly took a kinder tone toward him. "Look. I'm sorry about making fun of you. You alright?"

"Mhm," Koda hummed. He was not sure if he was lying. Mahuut made his bones rattle and his teeth clatter. He had never been around something that so obviously wanted to hurt him.

Teo looked as though he was about to say something nice, even smiling and stepping toward Koda. Then, he shrugged and said in a bored voice, "This room sure is bright." He traced the rays of light to oozy, amber bulbs hanging from the ceiling. They looked like bronze teardrops. Teo poked one of them with his sword. It made a squishing sound.

Koda smirked, "A booger!"

"A big, sticky booger!" Teo grinned. He broke into a trot, poking all the snot lights with his sword as he charged to the end of the chamber. Koda followed and both boys laughed as they entered the darkened room. They continued laughing until their eyes adjusted to the dim lighting. Then, they froze.

Teo's mouth fell. "Woah."

They had stumbled upon a gigantic feasting hall and were now staring at a massive banquet table. Seated at long benches were dozens of strange statues with rippling, rocky skin, and rough, grey features. Their limbs were wiry, twisty, and woody. Some had holes in their bellies and others had holes in their heads. A few had four arms and a few had only a single, fat leg. The boys walked around the table, staring at the assembly of stone.

"Their skin looks like bark," Teo remarked. "These were all trees!"

Koda gazed up at the statues. Their heads were adorned with headdresses made of tailored leaves. However, their treeish crowns were like their faces: petrified.

Teo rounded the table, passing under a grand chair. He wove through the legs of a kingly oak. In its thorny hands was a shattered scepter. Teo emerged from beneath the oaken throne and whispered, "I am starting to think this is Timbergrave."

"Mhm," Koda hummed. His heart was racing. He turned around. Light from the first chamber no longer penetrated the banquet hall. Instead, the light stopped before the archway, hitting something that was not quite a something at all. A shadow perhaps. Yet, a shadow that seemed to move of its own free will.

"Mahuut," Teo shuddered. The older boy rushed back and pushed Koda behind him.

A spirit took shape in the floorboards, a black cloud wafted toward the boys, and darksome tendrils licked their way through the hall—searching.

Teo put a hand on Koda's quivering shoulder. "It can't be worse than what was outside." He drew his sword and deepened his voice, "Leave us be, spirit. Or you will regret it."

The entity seemed to tilt a head, becoming a tall, gangly gloom. It approached them and to the boys' horror—the floorboards creaked. Teo pointed at the ground, at little pale threads emerging from the earth. "It must be a spider spirit. One of Mahuut's minions!" He lurched at the lurking legs, slicing them as they appeared.

This caused the gloom to groan and retreat to the corner. It growled as Teo closed in. It hissed when Teo raised his blade and shrieked when it was stabbed. Yet it did not strike back. It skittered onto the feasting table, fled toward the kingly oak, and crawled into the stony tree's lap.

Teo climbed onto the table from the opposite end. He stared the gloom down, sliced the air tauntingly, and marched forward. *Stomp. Stomp. Stomp.* Woodchips and dust rained onto the stone assembly. Koda saw at that moment that their branches were all held in front of their petrified faces. The statues were cowering. Realizing this, the boy gasped.

"What is it?" Teo barked. "More of them?"

"No," Koda replied. "No, no. It's just like the Hermit!"

"A lonely man and a vengeful spirit are two very different beings."

Koda did not think so. He stared at the slinking shade, which was pulsating and twitchy. It reminded him of a lost puppy, though far, far uglier.

Outside, the acid storm picked up again. Putrid raindrops began to pitter and patter. A hunting horn blew. Giant oars rowed overhead, creating violent gusts that hit the roof to the tune of *heave, ho, heave, ho.*

"Hear that?" Teo snarled. "It is summoning its master."

Koda glanced at his stained and sweaty clothes, *'Puppies don't always look their best in the pound.'* He blinked at the spirit. It did not look so shadowy anymore. Just dirty.

Teo crept toward the cowering spirit. He pointed his blade at the head-shaped part of the shadow.

Koda gulped and made a sudden decision. He sprinted toward Teo.

"Stay back!" the older boy ordered.

Koda ignored him, leaping at his waist. He swiped the canteen off his belt. He then ran to the gloom, unscrewed the cap, and splashed sweetwater onto it. The shadow recoiled, curling itself into a tight ball of pallid silks. Koda splashed it again.

Teo shrieked, "You're wasting it!"

The action was not wasteful in the slightest. The water washed over the gloom, soaking its silhouette in radiant waters. And what was more, the lamps in the hall suddenly lit up! The light pressed against the shadow. The dark veil condensed into a ball around the spirit. The gloom writhed up toward the ceiling, where it twisted and transformed. Black tendrils were severed. Creeping silks retreated beneath the floorboards. The darkness imploded in a dazzling display of color. Ghostly threads floated down like feathers; they folded upon themselves like worn clothes beside a bed.

THE TREE THAT DID NOT SLEEP

FROM THE GLOOM EMERGED a glowing sphere. It was blindingly bright for only a moment. Then, it lost its luster and the boys saw it: a large seed. It tumbled onto the oak's lap, bounced, and rolled toward the discarded threads of darkness.

Teo blinked in amazement. He then cheered at Koda and climbed down to hug him. "Nice job, kid. Who'da thought water would kill it?"

Koda stared in shock. He had not wanted to kill it. He craned his neck over Teo's beaming face. He waited breathlessly, hoping for some sign of life. At first, there was nothing—no movement, no sound. Then, there was the faintest crinkling of fabric; a lump grew within the scattered threads. The shadowy tatters were shed, falling like water off one's back.

The seed emerged and silks shot out from the seedpod, weaving into gossamer limbs. Twiggy toes in turn developed. Fernlike fingers followed. Finally, the top of the seedpod swelled and went, *pop,* sprouting a head without eyes.

"Oh, great," Teo groaned and grabbed his sword.

"Wait," Koda urged. "Remember the Hermit? We were scared of him, too. And he turned out okay."

Teo replied in a monotone, "I fail to see how this is the moment for a life lesson."

Koda walked in front of the older boy, pushing aside his sword. "We mean you no harm, spirit. We only want to find the great tree. Do you know where it is?"

The seedling spirit turned its head. Despite not having a face, it was clearly studying them. It threaded a silken stool of fine roots and sat, contemplating. It twirled the lonely leaf atop its head, like a child playing with its hair. Finally, it sent out a shoot of fine, bristly roots. It was as if the seedling wanted to shake Koda's hand.

"Don't touch it," Teo warned. "The Hermit is the one who told us to come here. This could all be an evil plan. They could be working for Mahuut."

Koda had not heard any thunder since the spirit had shown its true shape. There was no tap-dancing on the roof or heave-ho'ing of a hunting party. He shook his head, "You sound like my dad. He thought everyone was out to get him."

"Smart guy," scoffed the older boy.

Koda once thought so, too. And maybe in the real world, with its many faceless monsters, things *were* all bad. Maybe in the real world, it was best not to trust anyone. But Koda was not so sure about the spirit world. Although the seedling had no face, it looked at Koda as a friend would. Not like a monster. Not even like a human pretending to be nice. No, this was an honest spirit. Perhaps a little fearful, but Koda understood that (even more than he realized).

Without any further hesitation, he touched the seedling's roots. They wrapped around his hand. Energy surged through his arm, up his spine, and into his head. His eyesight shimmered. When it returned to him, it was not his own and he was no longer in the banquet hall.

He stood on a tall vista overlooking a mighty tree. The overstory must have stretched for miles. The organ-pipe trunks must have been wider than the seas that separate some countries. It was a place a god might live. The Banyan.

The giant tree's central trunk spiraled upward into a massive canopy. The branches stretched outward and in the humid air, aerial roots surveyed the ground. The oldest of these, nearest to the center, were like tree trunks themselves. They were thick with their own canopies and animals lived in those, too.

Squirrels hollered in their holes. Owls hooted in harmony with mourning doves. Monkeys ziplined across vines as jaguars tiptoed like trapeze artists. Even elephants had homes beneath the lower eaves—along with tapirs, rhinos, and other animals only the past remembers. And among all of this were trees wreathed in flowering crowns. They were walking.

Ancients, Koda awed.

Suddenly, his vision blurred. He was being transported somewhere. When he blinked, he was someplace where the air was warmer and the aerial roots thinner. The sun even managed to pierce the canopy in some places. Though, the sky was not clear. There was smoke above.

Koda's sight was turned toward the forest floor. Swarms of men were washing over the Banyan. Behind them was a tall, headless giant. Cradled in its hands was its own, severed head. It hooked the head to a fishing rod and cast it deep into the forest heart. At seeing this, the men below were sent into a frenzy. They chopped, sawed, and gnawed at the trees. Like dominoes, the aerial roots began to fall.

One by one, the canopy collapsed. The animals that lived in the tree scurried for shelter. Most did not escape and were sent in shackles to the headless giant. The Ancients fared worse. They were hunted and destroyed, from the largest to the least.

However, a few saplings and seedlings escaped by burrowing underground. There they waited in forgotten logs for a spring that never came. Eons passed before Koda like blurry images on a speeding train. Gradually, all the remaining tree spirits grew sleepy. They lost their leaves, their bark dried out, and one by one—they fell asleep forever.

———

"Wake up, kid."

Koda sat up, groggy from the vision. "Timbergrave *was* the Banyan! All these trees were just waiting for spring."

Teo helped him to his feet and said, dismissively, "That demon knocked you unconscious, kid."

Wounds which Koda forgot he had suddenly burned. He snapped, "Don't do that!"

"Do what?"

"Just because I am a kid doesn't mean I'm not smart. Or that you don't have to listen to me."

Teo raised his hands innocently, "I didn't say that."

"You implied it!"

"Fine," Teo agreed. "I'm just a stupid kid, too. Don't take me so seriously."

Koda licked the inside of his lips, unsure if he had won or lost the argument. He glared at Teo before turning to the seedling. "Mr. Tree Spirit, sir. We are trying to get to the Banyan. Is this all that is left?"

The spirit shook its head.

"Could you lead us to what remains?" Koda asked.

The seedling spun in a circle and sent its roots toward Teo. The warrior child leaped onto the table and yelled for it to stay back. Of course, it meant him no harm. It wove its branches into a complex shape. After a few moments, they saw that it was a canoe. Teo turned, "It's threatening us!"

"You dummy," Koda stated. "It's afraid. Just like you."

"I'm not afraid," Teo muttered.

"Your legs are shaking," Koda pointed. He walked toward the canoe. The roots reassembled into caricatures of Koda, Teo, and the seedling. One by one, each burst into white flames and became a gravestone.

"Now that's clearly a threat," Teo insisted.

To Koda, it clearly was not. He frowned at the trembling spirit. He wondered what an adult would say in his situation. Would his father tell the spirit to suck it up? Would he say there is nothing to fear? Both statements seemed wrong. So, he admitted, "You're scared and that's okay. I'm scared, too. Really scared."

The spirit retracted its roots and bowed its head. Koda smiled at it, "I'd be less afraid if you came with us, though. Maybe you'd feel better, too?" He smirked at Teo, "We have a sword master to protect us."

The seedling glanced at Teo; the stubborn boy looked away.

"Oh, come on," Koda persisted. "He's harmless."

The older boy put his arms over his chest and mumbled, "Nobody is harmless."

"Ugh. You're just like my dad."

"Yeah? Sounds like a swell guy."

"He's dead."

Teo took a step back. "I... I'm sorry. I didn't—"

Koda's mind went blank. It was the first time he had said that out loud. He did not intend to keep talking, but he could not stop his eyes from expressing themselves. First came a tear. It rolled down his cheek and was like the bursting of a dam. For the first time since his father had passed away, Koda mourned.

Teo cleared his throat, "Don't, uh. Don't do that. Hey. Look. Yeah, I can protect the tree." He approached the seedling. "We can be friends, right?"

The spirit observed him. After a moment, it waddled up and embraced him.

"Nice to meet you," Teo said through gritted teeth. He smiled at Koda, "See, kid. All better, right?"

It was not *all* better. The older boy was rude, stubborn, and brash. Yet, he was still kind in his own way. Koda wiped his eyes and strained a smile.

Relieved, Teo immediately pulled away from the seedling's hug. He changed the conversation. "I guess we need to find a way past Mahuut."

The seedling swirled around excitedly. Its many roots retracted and formed the image of a bag tied to a stick. The spirit rested the bindle on his shoulder and marched toward the far end of the banquet hall. The boys blinked at one another and ran after. They were led to an alcove in the wall, previously obscured by cobwebs and darkness. The seedling brushed them aside with his bindle, revealing an underground passage.

Teo began to turn, "I don't know about this. It might be—"

Koda would not hear it. He followed the tree spirit into the deep darkness without worry. He called back to Teo, "Be brave, kid. Be brave."

Teo's face swelled and he jogged after them. "I'll show you brave!"

THE UNDER ROAD

THE DESCENT WAS LONG and dark. The paths taken seemed random. To go down was often a case of going up. To go left was often a matter of going right. Yet, what was random to the boys seemed only sensible to their guide. For this was not a staircase but a root, and its route was reasonable to a tree.

Nevertheless, the boys struggled to follow. Stooping, squatting, and crawling were not easy things to do in the dark, especially for boys so badly equipped. Koda's hoodie constantly got caught on things and Teo's bare chest was sliced by unseen rocks. Presently, they were crawling through a crevice so narrow, a needle would have felt claustrophobic.

"Spelunking in the spirit world," Teo mumbled. "Didn't have that on my bingo card."

Koda did not reply. The humid air was hard to breathe. His lungs seemed congested and his windpipe felt as constricted as the crevice they crawled through. When they entered a new chamber, one which allowed his chest to fully expand, he paused to take some deep breaths.

Meanwhile, Teo reached for his canteen. In the depths, everything was amplified. Even silence had an echo down there. So, the clanking of his canteen, the unscrewing of the cap, and the subsequent spill were all quite audible. *Splash* went the sweetwater and off went Teo. He had quite the imagination where swearing was concerned. He invented several new words and expressions, most of which would make a woman blush—or slap him. Then, like a car running out gas, he sputtered to a stop and groaned, "I wish I had a lighter or something."

Hearing this, their guide waddled forward and transformed its bindle into a pale, glowing lantern. This did little to light their surroundings, but it was funny. And humor did much to brighten the mood.

From there, the journey was more relaxed and straightforward. They soon reached the bottom and entered a cavern flanked by rows of large stalagmites. These were hollowed out and fit with windows, doors, and balconies. Well-lit with cozy lights, the chiseled chambers gave all the hints of life. Yet aside from their echoing footsteps, all was quiet. All except a pair of voles.

They sat outside a stumped stalagmite on limestone stools. To their left were saloon doors and a sign that read *The Tap Root*. One vole chugged a sparkling beverage. The other read a newspaper. He relayed the news to his friend, "Seems some fisherlings have left the Banyan."

"How many?"

"The lodge says two. The warrens say three."

"They're sure they are fisherlings?"

"Nope. Doubt they're wanderers, though."

"Even if they are, so was Mahuut."

The other vole hushed him, "Don't say that name so loudly! How much have you had to drink?"

"Not nearly enough. Are you still going to Palimpsest then?"

"Unfortunately."

The boys passed the tavern and the voles' voices faded. Eventually, they came to a large, quartz door. It did not open when Teo or Koda pushed it. Yet, when their guide placed its hand on the crystalline handle, the ground tremored and the door groaned open. They entered a large chamber, wider and taller than any they had yet seen. The air was even more humid and despite having no trees, smelled woody.

Many spirits, roughly human in shape, had heard them coming. They were about Koda's height, and that meant short. What we might call their skin was a mix of colors. Some were blue, some were green, and some were red. Some were even colors that we have no words for. All of them wore wide and flattened hats. It was only once the boys were next to one of the workers that Teo exclaimed, "They're mushrooms!"

The workers all stopped. That was rather offensive and would be the equivalent of calling a human a monkey. Teo realized he had said something he should not have and cleared his throat. "Fungal folk?"

The attendants looked at one another, nodded, and went back to work. One of the fungal folk went to change a sign. He climbed up a ridiculously tall ladder. Every step he took caused glittering spores to float off the steps and surround his hands. When he reached the top of the ladder, the spores followed the movements of his fingers. They attached themselves to the sign and became neon letters that read: *Meadows to Palimpsest. ETA: 10 minutes.*

The boys supposed that was where their guide meant to take them. After all, no other arrivals or departures were listed. Teo and Koda found a bench while their guide talked to the workers. It seemed to be communicating through touch. From them, the spirit gathered that all terminals except for two were now inoperable. It also inquired whether the fungi had seen any other treelings.

Meanwhile, Teo finally apologized for earlier. "I'm sorry about your dad." His words echoed long after he said them.

"It's okay," Koda replied. He would rather not remember their conversation (or his father, for that matter).

"No. It isn't. I hate my old man, but I wouldn't want him to—you know."

Koda shrugged. He did not hate his father; he just disliked remembering him. Even when he was alive, his dad had been difficult to think about. He was even more difficult to talk about.

"How'd he die?" Teo asked.

Koda was quiet. On one hand, it really did not matter how his father had died. As the lady at the morgue had said, '*It's just clerical details.*' On the other hand, he felt he would be embarrassing his father by telling the truth: that his dad had died from a bunch of little, white pills in an orange bottle. "He was murdered."

Teo opened his mouth and then bowed his head. This was typically what happened when people heard about his father. Koda had already grown accustomed to it. Nobody knows how to respond to honest tragedy.

Then, Teo did something wholly unexpected. He kept talking. "So, is that why you feel like you don't have a home?"

"I don't *feel* like I don't," Koda replied bitterly. "I just don't."

Teo sent a gust of air through his lips. "Psh. You can make a home out of anything. You just need the right company."

Koda kicked his legs.

"What's wrong with your mom, anyway? A dad I can understand. But moms are, well. They're moms."

Koda shrugged. He had a reply in mind, one of those simple sentences that should be so easy to say. Those sentences, though, were the hardest for him. So instead, he told a half-truth, "She never came to see me. After my dad took me."

It was Teo's turn to go quiet. He contemplated the most tactful way to reply, going over a dozen renditions of the same general thought. At last, he raised his eyes in a friendly, *don't-be-mad-at-me* sort of way. "Did she know where you were?"

Koda glanced at Teo. He had asked that as if he knew the answer. Still, the boy would not give him the satisfaction of the full truth. "My dad moved us a lot."

"Fair enough," Teo replied. He rolled his shoulders and stretched his arms as if sentimentality was a coat to be taken off. He gestured at the tree spirit, "What should we name him? I think he looks like a Troy. Troy the tree."

Koda contemplated for a moment. Names were very important. Wanting one with meaning, he studied the seedling. Immediately, he was drawn to the lonely leaf atop the spirit's head. It reminded him of an old movie his father liked. "Alfalfa!" he exclaimed.

"Alfalfa?" Teo repeated.

Koda nodded.

"Like the character or the plant?"

"Both," the boy answered.

Now, Alfalfa had a name already, but it could not be said in any human language. I have tried to do so, and though I managed the first syllable by blowing air through my lips like a horse, the final seventy-five syllables were beyond me.

"Alright," Teo shrugged at the seedling. "I'm calling him Alpha, though."

The spirit was still conversing with the fungal folk. But an age had passed since it had used the Under Road. It had forgotten how gossipy its denizens were; they practically lived on darkness and decay. So much so, Alfalfa could not keep conversing. It was too dismal. The spirit took its leave and waddled back to the boys.

"Hi, Alfalfa!" Koda greeted.

"He's named you," Teo informed. "If that's okay?"

The spirit twirled its fernlike fingers in a delicate wave. It had received some sad news and was glad to have company.

Koda smiled at Teo, "I think he likes his name."

Alfalfa did enjoy his new name, although strictly speaking, *he* was not a he. Woodland spirits on occasion *do* wear pants and dresses, but this is only when the garments happen to get stuck on a branch. Nevertheless, as Alfalfa took no offense—neither shall we.

After exactly 9 and a half minutes (clocks in the Under Road ran a tad fast) a peculiar sort of train pulled up. There were no wheels, only gelatinous membranes that fixed the cars to the rails. And the tracks were not typical iron and wood, but a crystalline powder that wiggled and contracted as the cars went over it.

When the train finally stopped, a column of crimson spores billowed from the smokestack. The doors opened and various creatures stepped off the train. There were moles, voles, mites, and millipedes. There were also animals whose names are now long forgotten.

Teo stood up. "This is us."

Koda stared at the train. He felt like there was water in his lungs that he could not cough up. His shoulder ached from bruises he did not have. He shook his head and felt his eyes get heavy.

"Come on, kid," the older boy encouraged.

"Uh uh," was all he could muster.

Teo looked at the carriage. He hurried back to Koda and sat beside him. "Hey, this isn't the same train."

Koda's forehead was oozing sweat. His stomach was see-sawing. He stammered, "It can still crash."

Teo tried joking. "And so what if it crashes? We're already in the spirit world. Maybe it's like a board game and we just go back to the start."

"I'm not dead," Koda said emphatically. "And I'm not getting on that."

Teo had to think quickly. The train would not wait for them forever. He scanned the area for some inspiration. His gaze settled on the lead car. A tiny hand flicked a match out the window. A second later, smoke rings lazily lofted out the locomotive. Seeing those, Teo remembered that all trains have conductors. "Wait here," he told Koda and jogged away.

The conductor saw Teo coming from the window, staring at him as he huffed and puffed into the car only to look around confused. The boy swiveled his head in all directions, even glancing over the conductor once. "Where did he go?" He muttered.

The confusion, of course, was because the conductor was a prairie dog, and a girl at that. She wore a navy cap and was presently smoking a pipe. She had grey eyebrows and wore a permanent scowl. She glanced at his sword and blew a smoke ring up at him. "Bless me, a fisherling. Come to rob me?"

Teo jumped back. He had not seen her sitting there.

"You going to use that sword?" She blew a trio of rings at him.

Teo swatted them away, coughing. "I just need you to go really slow to..." He had forgotten the word of his destination, but that hardly mattered. The conductor would hear none of it.

"Need," puffed the conductor. "That's such a versatile word for your kind."

Teo blinked. "I just wanted to ask you to go a little slower for—"

"Oh, so now it's a want? Well, I grant you, that's more honest." She relit her pipe and pinched the flame of her match. Then, she flicked it at Teo's feet. "Pick that up."

"You flicked it," Teo muttered. "You pick it up."

The conductor mumbled to herself, exhaling smoke as she said, "Just as I figured. Well. So be it. Guards!"

"Please!" Teo insisted. "I'm not asking for myself. This is for my friend. He's scared to ride the train."

The conductor compacted the ash in her bowl. "And for that reason alone, I should delay my arrival? I should ruin the reputation of this fine locomotive and inconvenience every other passenger, some of whom may be in a hurry? Even for a fisherling, you seem conceited. You probably think the sun rises just to see you wake up."

Teo was ready to unsheathe his sword and *make* that train go slow. Just then, however, another prairie dog hopped onto the carriage. "What is all this commotion, Lucille?"

She blew more smoke in Teo's face. "This fisherling is overstaying his welcome."

"Alright, friend. Let's make some things clear, shall we?" The prairie dog tilted his head. "Wait, I remember you."

"Yeah," Teo smiled. "From the grasslands!"

"Yes indeed," the male prairie dog nodded. He looked at the conductor and stated frankly, "A rude one, this fellow. I'll see him off."

"No!" Teo said, raising his hands. "Please. The kid I was with. Remember him? He was in a horrible train accident recently and he's scared to get on."

"What an insult," the conductor muttered. "I've never hit a stray pebble. Let alone got in an accident."

"I believe you," Teo said (he did not). "But please, if you wouldn't at least go a *little* slower? It would help convince him to come aboard."

The conductor was now arguing out of general principle. Nothing Teo said would change her mind, for her mind was made. Fisherlings were trouble. She pointed the stem of her pipe, preparing to tell him off one final time. Then, Koda noticed what was happening and walked up to the locomotive. He recognized the prairie dog from the grasslands and called him by his name, "François?"

The prairie dogs were shocked in two ways: firstly, that Koda remembered François' name; and secondly, that the boy knew he belonged to it. They were used to humans, or fisherlings as they called them, confusing their kind for all sorts of animals. Most humans could hardly tell them apart from a ferret, let alone a white-tail from a black-tail.

Lucille put down her pipe and asked, "You are a friend to this boy?"

François was speechless, so Koda answered for him. "Mhm. He helped us a few days ago. What are you doing down here?"

"I should ask the same of you," grunted François.

"We met someone who would lead us to the tree. Do you take this train often?"

François shook his head, still shocked that a fisherling had remembered who he was. He said slowly, like a video playing at half-speed, "I've just come from Palimpsest on lodge business."

Though vague, that was true. François had been sent to investigate faraway happenings. Many animals, including the prairie dogs, had seen disturbing beings on their borders. Not just the boys, either. Dark spirits and malevolent creatures. Demons, some might call them. "The servants of Mahuut have been wandering farther than usual."

Teo looked at Koda, "See? He already rode the train, and he's just fine!"

"I'm more than *just* fine," François grumbled. "Lucille is the best conductor the Under Road has seen in generations!"

Lucille might have blushed, had the fur on her cheeks not gotten in the way.

François smiled at her and they shared a tender moment opaque to the rest of the world. Then, he walked to Koda and quietly asked, "Is it true you are afraid of getting on my *friend's* locomotive?"

Koda was speechless. "Not because I don't like her, or her train—it's just..." He could not talk about what had happened. For all he knew, everyone he had seen that day was gone. And perhaps, so was he.

François shuffled over to the conductor and conferred with her. They spoke quickly, with Lucille at one point raising her voice. François remained soft-spoken and gradually, Lucille's pipe died. She dumped the ashes out the window and began nodding rather than arguing. Finally, she looked at the boys and said, "I will reduce my speed by 15 miles an hour. Is this acceptable to you?"

They all looked at Koda. He felt the pressure to accept, to not be a coward. But he felt the pressure in his fearful heart, too—and that was still very great.

François leaned over, "Would you like that converted to kilometers?"

"No, it's okay," he said, voice shaking. He and the others did not know to which question he had responded. Neither did he for a time. Then, he exhaled. "I'll get on." He thanked Lucille for understanding, "You're really nice for doing this."

"Mhm," the conductor hummed, as if she begrudged him knowing so. "You two better not cause any trouble! Get on! We're already behind schedule."

As they boarded a passenger car, Teo asked, "Why did you help us, François?"

"Because I like your friend, and I hate to see a kind spirit darken. Too many do, these days." And at that, the prairie dog waved goodbye.

The Stops That Never Came

THEY FOUND ALFALFA SITTING alone. Teo offered a window seat to Koda. The child could hardly stomach being next to breakable glass. So, he politely refused.

It took about half the journey for Koda to adjust to the normal sensations and sounds. Every turn seemed too sharp. Every rattle seemed like a rocket launch. However, they were moving quite slowly. Eventually, he got comfortable enough to peek out the window. When he did, this is what he saw:

They were in a wide expanse. To call it a cave would be like calling a wall a fence. It was like a city flipped upside down. Rivers of gems ran across the roof. Pillars of earth-scraping stone plunged into the depths. A wide bridge occupied the center of the chasm. It was held up by giant roots from the roof above. They wrapped themselves in regular intervals around the bridge, suspending it in midair.

Koda looked ahead. He saw a massive, bearded face built of breathing roots. The bridge ran directly through its mouth. The beard swayed as the train neared. The structure's eyes seemed to move, watching them approach. Koda took a nervous gulp. The mouth got bigger and bigger and then—snap! They entered a dark tunnel.

"Want to go explore the other carriages?" Teo asked him. "I just saw one of the mushroom guys do it. Looks safe."

Koda craned his head. Unlike other trains, reaching the next car did not involve stepping outside. He wished it had, as it would have been easier to refuse. But it did not look dangerous and after a moment's hesitation, he agreed. Not wanting to be left out, Alfalfa went with them.

The three explored car by car. Few other passengers were on the train and most cars were empty. They found a few workers and several prairie dogs, but no humans. Then, they entered the caboose and were shocked by what they saw: dozens of seedlings and saplings all turned to stone. Some stood, holding onto poles. Others sat and looked out the window. A few had seeds in their palms and seemed to be holding them aloft in some sort of offering. Several fungal attendants were weaving between the entombed trees, dusting and polishing them.

"What happened to them all?" Koda whispered.

A voice came from behind. "After Mahuut's attack, they all left the Banyan." Startled, the boys turned and saw one of the voles who had been sitting outside *The Tap Root*. "They came down here to find a better life."

"So why are they still on board?" asked Koda. He watched as a worker scrubbed the feet of one of the petrified spirits.

The vole motioned toward the window. It was still too dark to see. "Many terminals were flooded or collapsed. But they're a stubborn folk, the Ancients. They all turned to stone waiting for stops that did not exist anymore."

The boys looked at one another and then at Alpha. Their guide approached one of the statues. Cradled in its rocky hand were nuts and acorns. The seedling delicately touched them. They immediately disintegrated.

"Died waiting for impossible destinations," the vole remarked.

Alfalfa walked to a larger statue, whose grassy hair was crowned in seedpods. Their guide reached out to take one of the pods and like before, the ashes of his kin slipped through his fingers. Koda tried to console the spirit, "It's so dark and dry down here. I bet we'll find more of your friends on the surface."

Alfalfa turned toward him and shrugged. His subsequent sigh caused the windows in the carriage to slide open. Just then, the dark cavern lit up. They pulled into a station almost identical to the one they had left.

"Well, this is my stop," stated the vole. "I imagine it is yours, too."

"Is this the Banyan?" Teo asked.

The vole stared at him strangely and shook his head. "Stay safe, you three."

It took some convincing to get their guide off the train. He would not leave until he had inspected every one of his fallen kin. He had to be sure they were not just sleeping. He had to be sure that, though time had forgotten them, he had not. When all his friends would not budge, when all their seeds had withered in his hands—Alpha finally left. Koda tried to hold the spirit's hand, but he pulled away.

Silently, they left the Under Road and climbed up a flight of sticky, smelly stairs. They surfaced above ground and took a breath that had no air in it. They looked around. It was bright, but it was not sunny.

Sure enough, they had made it to the Banyan. Yet, the fantastical tree was hardly a tree at all. Certainly not the one from their dreams. This was not the Banyan that had made a forest out of its own limbs, the tree whose shade animals had taken shelter in, whose crown was the home of kingly cats and birds.

This was no tree anymore. This was a city. A city of bones wrapped in sheet metal; a city whose trunks and branch-es were hollowed out into apartments; a city of blackened boughs that billowed smoke up to the roof of the world. There were no leaves atop the Banyan's crown, but there was a canopy. A canopy of foul clouds that rained soot onto their faces.

"How are we going to get home now?" The boys asked one another. Suddenly, they heard a thud behind them.

They turned to find their guide collapsed. The fate of his folk and the Banyan was just too much. His legs retreated into his seedpod. He resembled a turtle, with only his arms and head remaining visible. The boys nudged him and called his name, but the spirit was motionless. Nothing would bring him back. Slowly, the seedling began to petrify.

PALIMPSEST

As spirits are surprisingly heavy, they took turns carrying Alfalfa. Teo groaned, "We can't carry him the whole way. We need to wake him up." Koda agreed, though he did not know how. They tried shouting. They tried splashing sweetwater on his face. They even employed a few good slaps. Nothing worked. Eventually, they decided to find a doctor. Surely, the city had one of those.

It seemed to have everything else. The hazy streets were littered with grey, soot-faced spirits. They sold everything that could be bought and bought everything that could be stolen. Food (disgusting), drinks (dehydrating), furniture (deformed)—it all seemed to be sold in the understory. And at a discount! There were even thieves that tried to steal Teo's sword. Thankfully, there were also vendors that sold bandages for when they failed. But no doctors.

After walking through the ashen road, shaded by the hollowed trunks of dead trees, Teo had enough. He yelled at a street vendor—a painted, floating mask, "How can you not have any doctors here?"

The mask floated away. Nearby, a plump ooze of a man chuckled. Or, it would have been a chuckle if it had not become a coughing fit.

"What's so funny?" Teo growled.

"Ain't no need for doctors when nobody is sick."

"You just coughed," Koda commented.

"So?" the ooze-man replied, failing to see the correlation. "Only folks I know needs doctors now, live up in the canopy. Got too much sweetwater up there, make 'em all go loopy!" At that, he went cross-eyed and fell backwards in his chair. Whether he was giggling or choking, none could tell. He stared up at the sky and squinted, "Oh me oh my, is that the time? I'd best mosey back indoors. Y'all do the same, y'hear?"

"Why?" Teo asked, hand on his sword hilt.

The ooze-man closed the cabinets on his cart and rolled it away into the haze, giggling.

The boys stared at one another. Teo repositioned Alpha on his shoulders. He looked up at the ghostly apartments, whose dappled light shot through the haze like pale candlesticks in the sky. "I guess we find a way up there?"

Koda wiped the soot off his brow, "Anything is better than staying down here."

They continued toward the Banyan's center. The sun set and the roads cleared of vendors—all leaving in a hurry. At dusk, only the boys were on the road. Except, they did not feel alone. Their footsteps echoed more than they should have. The fronts of their faces felt cold, but the backs of their necks felt warm. And in the darkness, whispers slithered into their ears.

The boys did not say a word to one another. They both broke into a sprint. Neither knew how far they ran, nor for how long. Time moved strangely in the haze. It could have been seconds or minutes before they finally emerged from it. When they did, their echoes became their own again. They felt a welcome chill on their necks and a welcome silence in their ears.

"What was all that?" Koda shivered.

Teo said nothing and stared ahead, awestruck.

"What?" Koda asked before seeing it himself.

A massive surface root lay before them. It had been sliced across the middle, creating a flat ramp upon which giant ants rushed up and down. They wore great saddles but bore no riders. Teo pointed at a tunnel at the end of the ramp, where thousands of smaller trunks had been conjoined into one mighty base. "That's the only way I see us getting up the tree."

Exhausted and demoralized, Koda slumped down and shook his head. He wished now he had some sweetwater, anything to look forward to. More than anything, he wished the tightness in his throat would go away and he could get a proper breath. He looked up at the repurposed canopy, with its chimneys billowing black fumes into the air. "How can somewhere with all these fireplaces be so cold?"

Teo put the seedling down and sat beside Koda. He looked at the aerial roots all around him. He longed for the night sky he had taken for granted and frowned at those lit up limbs. "How can it be so bright without any stars?"

Koda glanced behind at the haze. "I feel like I am trespassing. Or—" He paused, thinking he heard something in the distance. "I feel like something is trespassing on me."

Teo frowned at Koda and, seeing the younger child was struggling, offered to help him to his feet. "Come on, kid."

"I don't want to," Koda whispered, though it was not his *want* stopping him. Rather, it was his fear. He expected Teo to call him names, but the older boy did not. Instead, he gave Koda his belt and with that—his sword.

"I don't know how to use that," said the child.

"Neither do I," Teo admitted.

"Don't you need it?" Koda asked.

"Nah," dismissed the teenager. "Nobody will mess with me. As my father says, I am naturally abrasive."

"Oh, okay," Koda replied, not knowing what *abrasive* meant. He tied the belt in a knot around his thick hoodie. Teo helped him adjust the hilt so it would not whack him as he walked. Then, he stepped back and admired his work.

"There we go! You're a warrior, now." He smirked at the boy's baggy shorts, "With a kilt and all!"

Koda wobbled as he took his first steps. "I feel stupid."

"That's fine," Teo told him, picking Alfalfa up for an extra turn. He slung the spirit's arms around his shoulders like a backpack. "As long as you feel brave, too."

Koda wanted to argue yet found he could not. You see, one does feel stronger with a sword at one's side—even if one's hands are too shaky to use it.

They came to the foot of the Banyan, where ants raced up and down their highway. Now up close, they saw just how large the ants were, and how quickly they moved. Not wanting to be trampled or worse—eaten—the boys hesitated. "Maybe there's another road?" Koda asked. "For people like us?"

There was another road. It went down, rather than up. It led to a shanty town built into the base of the ramp. Located in a natural depression, the air sank into a thick layer of smog. There, the makeshift houses were stacked atop one another. But the boys would not have known this. They saw only the topmost floors, floating as if on a misty sea. Welcoming lights lit up the buildings and Koda wanted to stop there for the night. "That man warned us to get indoors."

Teo was wary and noted, "Do *you* see anyone in that village? Do you hear anyone?"

Koda squinted. There were no faces, there were no voices. All he heard was the whining of rusted metal. The only movement came from a porch swing, slowly rocking in the breeze. Yet there was no wind. "Maybe everyone's asleep?" Koda suggested, though he did not believe it.

"We can't go in there," Teo decided. "We've got to go up." He hiked back to the highway, ignoring Koda's calls to slow down. When he reached the base of the ramp, he raised his arm and waved at the bugs.

"They're not horses," Koda hissed.

Teo ignored him. He snapped his fingers and hollered at an oncoming ant. It noticed them and left the flow of traffic. Koda reached clumsily for his sword, but by the time he had a grip—it was too late. Or, it would have been if the ant had not lowered itself onto its belly, tilted to its side, and given them an easy way to climb up. Teo looked back, grinning.

Koda shook his head in disbelief. The ant had been hailed like it was a taxi. A vicious, man-eating, insectoid taxi.

Teo pushed Alfalfa up and then climbed onto the saddle. He offered a hand. "There's more than enough room! Hop on!"

Koda swallowed. He flashed a look at his new sword and took Teo's hand. The saddle was larger than it looked and fit them comfortably. Koda held onto Alfalfa, who was wedged behind Teo. At first, the older boy did not know where to put his hands. Then, he confused the ant's antennae for reins. Luckily for him, that was exactly what their mount was waiting for. The ant burst to its feet and *zip*! They were off!

The insects swarmed through the streets effortlessly, requiring no stoplights, signs, or separate lanes. Once inside the Banyan's hollow trunk, the traffic funneled into a spiraling highway. The road went up and up, narrowing into a dot of light.

As they ascended, circling and circling, up and up—the boys' stomachs came closer to their mouths. After minutes of dizzying spirals, Koda asked, "How will it know where to go?"

Teo leaned forward and matter-of-factly inquired, "Can you take us to a, uh, a place for spirits?"

The ant promptly halted. The traffic flowed around them like water passing a pebble. Teo began elaborating, explaining that they needed a place for a 'sick' spirit. While he did that, Koda watched the marching ants. He thought, *'Why are they saddled if nobody is riding them?'*

Then, he turned his head in just the right way. Hazy lamplight from a nearby exit filtered in, illuminating the dusty air. Outlined in the dust were silhouettes of men and women, barely visible were it not for the polluted air. Their ears were shrunken and their noses were flat. Yet, their eyes were wide and hungry. Their tongues wagged out open mouths like those of wild dogs.

Suddenly, their ant scampered for the nearest exit. Within seconds, they were surrounded by a city unlike any they had ever seen. They had entered the Nodules: a neighborhood stitched out of the Banyan's open sores. These were mansions, tumorous and toxic—with gilded doors fitted onto hollowed galls. They were treasure hoards, mostly—with too many rooms and too few beds, too many windows and no light to let in.

As they went higher up the canopy, the branches thinned out. They left the Nodules and entered a shanty. Though, this neighborhood was far more sprawling and chaotic than the one below. The boys could not tell where one house ended and another began. Rooftops were floors, walls were doors, and everywhere was everyone's.

Yes, I am afraid to say the boys had entered a proper slum. It was equipped with all the amenities one expects from such an establishment: greedy landlords, cramped conditions, dangerous diseases. Poltergeists warmed their hands beside burning trash cans. Sludge monsters slurped slop off the street. And everywhere the boys looked, eyes in faded bodies watched them like drawings that had been erased.

Fortunately, there was one small branch on the Banyan that was different from all the rest. It was that branch the boys were now bound for. It took some time weaving through the slums to reach it, but by midnight the setting did change. The air grew cleaner. The street widened slightly and calmed significantly.

At the end of the road, at the very tip of the branch, was a single home. The boys could see only its silhouette. Even from the opposite end of the road, it seemed big. Yet as they approached, they could not get a better look because of a tall hedge that walled the property off. They did, however, see a humble cottage—a gatehouse of sorts—wedged between the hedge. It was built of redbrick and covered in crawling ivy. To its right was a wrought-iron gate.

The ant approached the gatehouse. It lowered its belly to the ground, signaling the journey was over. Teo slid nimbly off their mount with Alpha on his back. Koda followed after, managing a controlled fall. He offered a breathy, "Thank you," to the ant. From how long the insect lingered and how it huffed when it left, it likely would have preferred money.

"This is a weird hospital," Teo muttered.

As if in reply, the door to the gatehouse flapped open, spewing leaves like spittle. "Welcome to Palimpsest Sanatorium. Entry fee, please."

Teo blinked three times in confusion. He turned to Koda and frowned, "Sorry, kid. I don't know why I thought the ant would know what 'hospital' meant. Let's get out of here."

The gatehouse door knocked repeatedly against its hinge. "Palimpsest Sanatorium is the premier facility for all spiritual ailments. From hospice to memory, let us take care of your sluggish, insolent, or otherwise insolvent spirits."

Teo craned his head, trying to peek over the hedge. "Hm." He looked back at Koda, "The house past the hedge does look nice."

"Our facilities are state of the art," blabbered the brick structure. It left out the rather obvious fact that the state of art in those areas left much to be desired.

Teo scrounged his pockets for loose pennies. He found only an exceptionally preserved piece of lint. "But we don't have any money."

The gatehouse opened its wooden door. A gust of wind blew from the parlor room within, becoming a series of elegant insults best left unsaid.

Koda interjected, "Why have a hospital at all?" He remembered what Alfalfa had shown him and what Mahuut and his men had done. The Banyan he had seen did not need hospitals. "You've already ruined the tree. Why not just let everyone be sick?"

The gatehouse went silent. The shutters on the windows flapped open and closed. "Why, little one. Then, we could not take your money!"

Koda was stunned. "That's horrible! You, you—You can't do that!" He could not believe he was arguing with a house about right and wrong.

"That's..." The gatehouse trailed off, making a hissing noise. He then finished the thought abruptly. "How it is here."

Teo shook his head, "So you destroy the Banyan and—"

"Dear children," the gatehouse interrupted. "I do not have the time to explain economics. I am but a humble house with a gate. Please provide patronage or depart."

Thus began a fierce bickering between the boys and the building. While they were arguing, a woman came out of the Sanatorium. She carried a basket to the hedge, intending to gather some grapes for her patients. But when she heard the commotion, she went over to the gatehouse. She overheard Teo explaining, "We have a sick spirit."

The gatehouse was quiet for a moment. Then, it stated, "Have you considered Palimpsest Sanatorium for your memory care needs? Entry fee, please."

Teo licked his lips, stunned. "Did a house just call me stupid?"

"Forgetful," Koda corrected. "But, yeah."

Teo took a big breath of mean words, but the woman on the other side of the hedge interrupted him. "Pardon me, Hedginald. These three are my new workers. The entry fee should not apply to them."

The gatehouse innards shuffled as if someone were pacing within. The wrought-iron gate to the boys' left whined open. The woman poked her head out and waved them over, "Come on, you three. You're late. You'll have to sleep on the floor, for that."

Teo stared shamelessly, for she was the most beautiful woman he had ever seen. She had long, red hair and green eyes, but most captivating was her smile. It sat perfectly still between her high cheekbones and dimples, never quite leaving—even in a frown. It was that smile that so enchanted Teo. Without any reservations, he followed her through the hedge. Koda was less convinced. Pretty women were rarely nice and nice women were always accompanied by mean men. Yet, as he preferred not to bicker with bricks, he eventually followed, too.

"Thank you, ma'am," said Teo in a tone Koda had never heard from him before.

The woman nodded and said nothing. Once they were far from the gatehouse, the woman turned to them. "You must forgive me for Hedginald. He takes his job too seriously, but it is important to seem cruel. In Palimpsest, helping others is seen as a weakness."

Teo scratched his head. "What about fees, taking people's money? That was a lie?"

"A clever use of honesty."

The boys glanced at one another. Koda pointed to the seedling on Teo's back, "Our friend is sick. Can you help him?"

The woman set her basket down and looked at the petrified spirit. She gasped, "An Ancient!" She peered at the boys and inquired, "However did you find one?"

Teo tried to say something heroic or mysterious. Instead, he blurted, "Walking."

The woman laughed. "And what is this little one's name?"

"Alfalfa. I'm Koda and this is—"

"Teo," the older boy declared, raising his shoulders to appear brawnier.

"Those are all beautiful names." She stared at them, saying nothing for a few seconds. Then, she reminded them of their manners. "Aren't you going to ask me for my name?"

Teo began to stutter. Koda took a step back, thinking she was scolding them. Neither boy knew what to say until she smiled at them. After that, everything became calm and easy. The boys asked in unison, "What's your name?"

Mom's Sanatorium

"I GO BY MANY names in these late years. The far-off folk know me as Whispers-in-the-Wind. The Ancients used to call me... Well, it was a frightfully long name that involved whooshing sounds and popping one's lips." She giggled to herself, "They told me it translates to She-Who-Readies-the-Soil."

"That's an interesting name," said Teo.

"It's much better than what most folks in Palimpsest call me."

"Palimpsest?" Koda repeated. He kept hearing that word. It was a big one that even adults never used.

"The name for the Banyan, or at least what Mahuut left of it." The woman ushered them up the steps of a pillared porch. She opened a faded, red door and led them into a beautiful drawing room. The walls were lined with fern wallpaper, the couches were capped in bronze, and the coffee table had a built-in chessboard. Two spirits were sitting around a fireplace. "Hello, Damu. Hello, Artio."

The spirits barely looked up, though the healer took no offense. She grabbed a poker from beside the fireplace and turned over one of the logs. Meanwhile, the boys analyzed their surroundings. A staircase with a silver railing led to a loft. Ghosts had gathered there to see the new arrivals. They shimmered and scowled, their shadows wagging in the firelight.

"Most of my patients don't talk much and when they do, it can be hard for them to express how they feel." She led them to the kitchen, saying, "Most of them just call me Mom. You're free to do so, too."

Teo had no issue with that. However, Koda did not want to call her by any name, especially that one. "You aren't our mom."

The woman knew perfectly well why the child had said that (even if *he* did not). "You may call me whatever name you are comfortable with, Koda."

So amazed by her calm and kind response, Koda quickly got embarrassed. He mumbled a moment later, "Mom is fine."

"Perfect." She washed her hands in a marble sink. The faucet was the shape of a dragon's head.

"That's a cool sink," Teo remarked.

"It's not really my style," Mom told them, getting her hands good and soaked. "But that dragon's head is the only thing that can filter the water here. Alright, that should be wet enough. How about we see to Alfalfa?" She walked them past the kitchen into a solarium full of exotic plants. The walls were made entirely of glass and a pond was in the corner.

Mom sat with Alfalfa at the edge of the pond. She held his hands in hers. The purified water went from her fingertips to his. Within a moment, the seedling's earthly brown complexion returned. A little white root wiggled out of his body and curled around Mom's hair. "Welcome to my home, Ancient One."

The boys were confused. "He just needed water?"

The Ancient's root retreated into its seedpod. A fog of grey covered Alpha once again. Frowning, Mom put a hand on the spirit's head and patted it. She whispered something to the seedling and set him down. "Water is always a good start, but I am afraid his sorrow will not easily wash away."

Teo grumbled, "We had to carry him all this way because he was sad?" Mom stared at him with disappointment, causing him to look away. He mumbled, "Maybe I should have given *him* my sword."

The seedling hardened. The seedpod became a stone shell from which light bounced off. Mom frowned, "Your friend was born in the old world, with promises of green country and pleasant soil. You found him hiding in some forgotten tomb, no doubt? I thought so. I do not think a sword can help him face the future he finds himself in."

Koda squinted, "I thought you were a healer?"

Mom did not react to his rudeness. She looked at him and answered, her open eyes piercing his narrow gaze: "Sadness is a hard thing to heal. The only medicine that works is the stuff we give ourselves."

Koda slumped against a mossy stone and massaged his scalp. "What do we do now?" Of all the places they had seen in the spirit world, Palimpsest was the worst. And the Sanatorium was not much better. It reminded him of his brief stay in a foster home (which is where he learned the meaning of *oxymoron*).

Teo shook his head. He lifted his canteen, drinking the rest of the sweetwater until only droplets remained. Craving another mouthful, he peered into the container. Mom saw this and gently took the canteen away. "I will take care of your friend."

Koda blinked, not sure which friend she meant. He had been referring to the Banyan anyway. Whatever Palimpsest was now, it was not the tree they had hoped would lead them home. "I meant about—" He cut himself off, unsure whether he could trust the woman.

Teo finished the thought without worry. "We both had a vision about this tree. Or what this tree once was. It was supposed to take us home."

Mom went to the kitchen, filled the canteen, and handed it back to Teo. He drank from it immediately and gagged. "This is regular water."

"*Thank you* is the correct response. Purified from that faucet you were admiring."

Teo coughed up some manners, "Oh. Uh. Thank you, Ma'am."

Mom walked the perimeter of the solarium. She took a wilted sunflower into her arms. At that moment, the boys realized all the plants there were sick. "It is important to be hopeful. This city may yet lead you home."

"But how?" Teo asked, clipping the canteen to his side.

Mom looked at him thoughtfully. Not even a sword could have cut as deeply as her stare. "Some destinations are reached by taking detours."

That made a lot of sense to Teo. Unfortunately, he was too tongue-tied to make much himself. To say he was enchanted would be like—well, actually that would be quite right. He was enchanted.

Koda was less so. He had not asked to be whisked away to some magical world. He especially had not asked for the opinions of some crazy lady. "Any tips? Any detours you'd suggest?"

Mom peered through the window. "The spirit world is a mysterious place. I would think the Heartwood has a part to play in all this."

"The what?"

"The Heartwood. The uncorrupted core of the Great Tree. Not even Mahuut has found a way in there." She grabbed Alfalfa, an empty ceramic pot, and a bag of soil. "It is at the bottom of the Banyan, behind an impenetrable wall of vines."

Koda and Teo glanced at one another. *"The hollow?"* Koda mouthed. Teo shrugged and clarified, "Impenetrable, you said?"

"As of now, yes. But do not despair. There is enough of that already." She covered the seedling in soil and placed his pot back on the pond, facing east. "Besides, a couple of good-natured kids is just what this city needs."

Teo's cheeks were so red that they could have been confused for ripe tomatoes. His voice cracked, "You think I'm—we—are good-natured?"

"Why should I not?"

Teo blinked several times and stuttered. "Uh, well. Hm. Right."

For a few days, the boys (mostly Teo) were happy to help Mom with chores. Their first morning, they gathered grapes. Koda thought it would be a simple task. As it turned out, the grapes were awfully talkative and quite clever, always bargaining for one more night on the vine. One even tried to bite him! On another occasion, the boys cleaned the chimney. The resulting cloud of soot soon gained sentience and demanded to see Mom. Thankfully, it only wanted a cup of chamomile tea for the road.

Yes, there was always something going on. The Sanatorium was a revolving door of mischief. The patients ranged from mildly loony to utterly insane. On their second day, a feathered serpent tried to burn itself alive. Mom scolded it for that. "Queztal, what did I say about being that close to the fireplace?"

The serpent hissed, reminding its caretaker about all the great empires that had worshipped it.

Mom put her hands on her hips. "Don't get prideful with me. Must I remind you that before men worshipped gods, gods worshipped me? Now go on and wash for supper."

That was not even the worst of the commotion. On the third day, Teo beat a spirit named Eris at chess. This proved to be a mistake, as she grew incredibly angry and threatened to start a war in the drawing room. Luckily, Mom came by and consoled her, though the boys were warned not to fall in love for a few days.

"Why?" Teo asked, worriedly.

Mom only chuckled. She was used to her patients' quirks.

Koda was not. On the fourth day, when he went to get water for Alfalfa, he found there was no faucet on the sink. The dragon's head had vanished. He asked Mom where a faucet could have run off to. She sighed, grabbed a jacket, and went outside to an adjacent pond. Thus began an hours-long debate between her and a spirit named, "Hebo," during which time they had no access to clean water. It took until midnight for the spirit to come back inside. By then, Koda and the plants were nodding off.

"Still awake?" Mom asked.

Koda wiped the drool off his chin and looked around. Mom was tending to the plants. Yet, the water she poured pooled in the pots. The wilted stems did not stand up. He told her, "You're overwatering them."

"They don't like to drink when people are nearby," Mom replied. "They begrudge every happy sip I give them." She pointed to the sickly sunflower, "That one won't drink until I go to bed."

Koda looked at Alfalfa's pot. Like the other plants, the petrified seedling had yet to drink. "Why are they so stubborn?"

Mom put her watering can beside Alfalfa. She then answered slowly so that Koda had to follow her to the kitchen to listen. "They all have their reasons. Some I agree with more than others. All I empathize with." She gestured to a seat at the table.

"I'm okay," Koda declined.

Mom shrugged and started washing dishes. After a few plates and pans, she declared like a narrator in a storybook: "Alfalfa, the tree that would not drink. And Koda, the boy who would not sit."

He bit the sides of his cheeks. "I'm not being like Alfalfa. I want to keep going."

"And for that, I am glad. Though to where are you going, I wonder?"

Koda glared, "Home."

"Is that right?"

"Yes," Koda blurted.

"Hm."

Koda sucked in his bottom lip, licking it.

Mom turned off the faucet and dried her hands on a washcloth. "Thank you, Hebo." She sat at the kitchen table and patted the chair next to her.

Koda again refused. "I'm tired."

"Want to go to bed?"

He shook his head hesitantly.

"Then sit."

Had anyone else said that, Koda would not have listened. And yet there was no sharpness in her voice, no command. Only pity. Pity that could mow down a mountain. And so, Koda sat.

"There we are. Tea? Coffee?"

Koda stared into his lap. "Why do you pretend to be a mom?"

"I *am* a mom. Why do *you* pretend to hate me?"

"I don't pretend to." He looked up and corrected, "And I don't hate you. It's just—" He started fidgeting. Not the kind of fidgeting done by an idle mind, either. Rather, a mind that was overflowing. He held his hands as if he feared he would lose them. He rubbed his forearms as if to hug himself. His legs bounced anxiously, he started to stammer, and—

Mom took his hands. When he unconsciously balled them into fists, she slowly and gently uncurled his fingers. Softly, she asked, "Can you go to the solarium and get my watering can?"

Koda did not know why she wanted it now, nor why he had to get it for her. Still, he was glad for a reason to get up. He went and sat by the pond for a moment, on a stack of red flagstone. After a few deep breaths, he glanced at Alfalfa. The seedling was inert like the stone they both sat on. And yet, as Koda peered—he noticed something peculiar. Alfalfa's pot had drained. All the plants had drunk, in fact. Even the stubborn sunflower had taken a few sips.

Koda returned with the watering can. He set it on the table and stepped away.

"Still a 'no' on tea?"

"I'm good."

The healer turned her chair toward him. "A word of advice, then?"

"Uh. Sure?"

"I know a thing or two about the soul, Koda. More than enough to see that a darkness hunts you. It will not stop until you defeat it."

"You mean Mahuut?"

"Mahuut may have a part to play, yes."

Koda raised his hands and shrugged, "Got any suggestions?"

"I do not." She narrowed her eyes, "But I will say this: We all wish our world was brighter. Don't keep yourself in darkness because you will not open the blinds."

All was quiet. Had there been crickets, this would have been their cue. Mom yawned and pushed in her chair. "Well," she said in that singular tone that always meant goodbye. "I think I'll go to bed. Goodnight."

Koda knew when he was being taught a lesson—even if he did not know what it was. The child looked back at the solarium. "Goodnight."

The healer left him to his thoughts. These being poor company, Koda walked off as well. He contemplated sitting in the drawing room, but all the comfy chairs were taken. Moreover, the couch was occupied by two spirits engaged in a staring contest. And as they had neither eyes nor mortal lifespans, Koda figured they would be there a while. Reluctantly, he went upstairs.

Their bedroom was the last one on the right and was the only room that could be locked from the inside. It was sparsely decorated. Aside from a dresser full of clothes and a desk full of cobwebs, there was only a bunkbed in the corner. The sole redeeming quality was the ceiling, which twinkled like the night sky.

Presently, Teo wore a pair of pajamas that had once belonged to a poltergeist. They caused his body to hover. So, he slept on the top bunk. He was staring at the ceiling stars when Koda entered. "Where've you been?"

Koda swallowed. "Watering things."

"Ah... Hey. I was thinking. Maybe the Hermit was right?"

Koda was taken aback. "What?"

"About our vision, that is." He sat up excitedly, "Maybe we had it all wrong and we weren't supposed to go back. Maybe this is supposed to be our home."

Koda was unsure. He was thinking again about Miss Wellington. He hoped she was okay. But she was not the only woman he was thinking about now. He wondered about his mother. His real mother. Try as he might, he could not picture her face. And for the first time, that made him very sad.

"What's wrong?" Teo questioned. He floated above his bunk like a genie on its cloud.

"Don't you want to go back?"

Teo thought hard about his response. Like Koda, he too had few friends. "I don't know," he replied. "This is a big city. We might have family here. Uncles, aunts, grandpas. Pets."

"Pets?"

Teo's face darkened. "Just an example." He turned over and pulled the covers past his face. He curled into the fetal position. "All good dogs go to heaven, right?"

"And this is heaven?" Koda snorted.

Teo growled, "I don't know, kid. Why are you interrogating me, huh? And why are you so eager to go back to your own life? You sure made it sound lousy."

"It was," Koda argued.

"Then why not just..." Teo sighed and trailed off.

Koda did not press the subject because he had a point. And yet, something had changed. He went to his bunk and pulled the duffel bag out from beneath the bed. He took out one of the old man's paints, a half-empty titanium white. He twisted the cap. As ever, it remained shut. He tried bending, biting, and breaking open the tube. All attempts failed.

The room was quiet for several minutes. And yet, the private thoughts of each boy seemed to make the silence louder. Finally, Teo muttered, "I think we could be comfortable here. Happy."

Those words were eerily familiar, though Koda took a second to remember why. Suddenly, he recalled that day at the Cabin. He heard the Hermit's voice: *One can only use these paints if one is content. Comfortable. Happy.*

"But you don't agree," Teo whispered.

Koda put the paint in his hoodie pocket and collapsed onto the bed. "I guess not." For the first time since entering the spirit world, he yearned to sleep.

THE BOY THAT WOULD NOT SIT

EVERYTHING WAS WHERE IT was supposed to be. The dream never changed. Koda sat on the floor of a ransacked bedroom, head bowed. His mattress was leaning against the wall. His sleeping bag was ripped open.

"You think it's funny to hide my stuff?" His father snarled. "Go on, explain yourself! You get a rise out of my pain?"

Koda barely managed a whisper, "I don't like it when you take your medicine."

His father dangled an orange pill bottle. "Well too bad, kid. And because of all the stress you've caused me, I'm going to have to take double!"

Koda looked up. He dared a final reminder, "The bottle says you can only take two a day."

"Should have thought about that before you put me through the ringer!" He threw four pills into his mouth, leaned forward, and gulped them down with a devilish smile. "Ah! Much better."

Koda woke from his nightmare, panting. He turned over and eyed Teo enviously. The older boy had kicked off his covers and was snoring in mid-air, occasionally bumping into the ceiling like a balloon.

With a sigh, Koda left the bedroom. He returned to the solarium. There was no trace of water in any of the pots. The soil was bone-dry. The solemn sunflower was resting its wilted head on a bare-branched bougainvillea. A lone-leafed lemon tree wore a scarf of sickly pothos. Jade leaves fell like the ticking of a clock. *Click. Click. Click.*

Koda sat beside the pond and held Alfalfa's pot. The spirit looked even worse than the day before. He had sunk deeper into the soil and the leaf atop his head had shriveled up. However, when the sun rose, the leaf twitched toward the light. This made Koda hope for a fairy-tale reawakening. When none came, he put down the petrified seedling. "I can't wait for you to get better."

Then came a moment that lasted for an hour. As the jade leaves ticked and tocked, Koda lost himself in a singular thought. He fidgeted with the spell-locked paint in his pocket. All the while, he bit his cheek.

Sometimes, you do things without realizing them. You make a decision and only after the fact, find you have made it. And just like that, you find yourself doing something wholly unexpected. This is what happened to Koda. He had not planned to go out onto the porch. And when he did, he surely did not plan to keep going. And yet he did—down the porch steps and all the way to the hedge gate. It was there he saw a familiar face.

Mom stood behind the gate, arms gliding through the air in a rhythmic dance. Behind the hedge, a wall of brown smoke had gathered. As Koda neared, he saw that it was no ordinary smoke either. Within it were hollow eyes and sagging mouths. Arms and legs without bodies climbed up the hedge.

Koda stared at the gaseous horror and then blinked at Mom. Her arms remained in constant motion. Her face never blinked. As he approached her, the clamor of the gas cloud seemed to quiet. In its place was Mom's voice, though not as it was the night before. It had overtones, like a choir unto itself. She was chanting, and though Koda did not know what she was saying—he could tell what she was doing.

The noxious fumes shrank. Light pierced the shadows. Gusts knocked the climbing limbs back down. Then, clasping her hands, she uttered a final prayer. The wind howled, blowing out the haze like candles on a cake.

And thus the cloud dispersed. The sun shone down. Its rays were a spotlight within which Koda stood. He squinted at the woman in awe.

Mom fell to her knees, exhausted. It took her a minute to notice Koda. When she did, she jumped and grabbed her heart. "Oh—Koda! I didn't see you there." She giggled, "No wonder that went better than usual."

"That happens all the time?"

When Mom spoke, it was as if she had aged. She was still beautiful, but time had carved chasms across her skin. Crows had buried their feet in her eyes. "Occasionally."

"Was that... Mahuut?"

"M'yes. Awfully persistent today, though I suspect that is because of you."

"Me?"

"And Teo," Mom added between breaths. "And Alfalfa, if he knows about him."

Koda suddenly had phlegm in his throat. He swallowed it to no avail. Only when he spoke did his throat clear. "If I wanted to leave, would you be mad?"

The woman cocked her head. "Why would you think that?"

"Because... This place is safe? Because you want us to be happy?"

"Koda, my friend—I have no power to give happiness." She stood up and in the dappled sun, seemed more youthful. "This is a sanatorium. Once you are healthy, you leave."

Koda swallowed again and glanced at the ground. "So, you wouldn't be mad?"

"I'd be proud, actually."

The boy looked up, thinking he was being insulted in some way. Pride was something people had for others, not him. He tried to speak; no words came out. All he could manage after several breaths was an airy, "Why?"

The caretaker stared at the sanatorium. "We are all trying to find our home, Koda. When we do not see it on the horizon, many of us give up and get lost."

"I'm still lost," Koda reminded her and himself.

"No," Mom smiled. "I do not think so."

Koda gazed at the caretaker. For the first time, he saw what Teo had always seen. She was a light that did not cast a shadow, an echo that did not distort. She was pure. The realization made him smirk.

Like a reflection, she smirked back, "What is it?"

"I want to say sorry for how rude I have been to you. But since you know a thing or two about the soul, it's probably not necessary."

Mom put her hands on her hips and chuckled. "What a roundabout way of apologizing anyway." She opened the wrought-iron gate, causing Hedginald to wake up.

"What's all this? Welcome to Palimpsest. Entry fee, please."

Koda glanced at Mom worriedly. She chuckled and shook her head. "No fees yet. But Palimpsest is a greedy place. You'll be asked to pay for things at every turn. And not just with money."

A ray of light shot through the window and without covers to hide under, Teo was soon wide awake. He swam through the air, toward his dresser, and changed into his normal clothes. At that moment, he thought only one thing: he had overslept. If he did not hurry, someone else might make breakfast for Mom. He jogged downstairs and went outside to gather herbs.

He immediately noticed Koda and Mom near the hedge. Feeling a little jealous, he came over and questioned, "What's going on?"

"Your friend is going to find a way into the Heartwood," Mom answered. "Isn't that right?"

Koda had not thought much about his next steps. Though, he supposed that was the sum of it. He nodded, "I want to go home."

The teenager lifted his brow. "I thought you didn't have one?"

Koda shrugged and started to explain. Teo interrupted him, "Eh, whatever. You pack your sword?"

The child frowned.

Teo wagged a finger. "I thought so. Hold on." He ran back inside and returned with the sword. He handed it to Koda and patted his back. "Good luck, kid."

"I think you should go with him," Mom suggested. Her voice was like a rose, lovely yet sharp.

Teo's heart sank in his stomach. "You do?"

"You do?!" Koda repeated, twitching a smile.

"Of course. After all, this is not your home."

Teo cleared his throat. He had hoped it would be. "I don't mind the pollution."

"I do."

Suddenly, Teo's face changed. He looked away, scowling. He deepened his voice. When he spoke, it cracked anyway. "I guess I'll go, then."

"Perfect!" Mom exclaimed.

Teo stated like a warning, "Right now. Without breakfast or anything."

"That would make me very proud!" the woman encouraged. "Of both of you."

Teo licked the inside of his lip. After a brief silence, a sort of standoff with the woman, he whirled around and growled. "Come on, kid. Let's go find ourselves a hole to crawl into."

And so the pair passed beyond the hedge. As the gate shut, the healer gave them one last bit of advice (though only Koda listened). "Be careful in Palimpsest. Much will be asked of you. And few can pay the Fisherman's Tithe."

THE DEAD MAN'S DIRGE

THEY DECIDED TO TRY their luck and rode an ant taxi to the bottom of the Banyan. Or, *almost* to the bottom. Their mount halted once the air grew cold and would go no further. So, the boys thanked the ant (who, again, would have preferred money over words) and walked down the cobwebbed road.

They circled the trunk for the last time, descended the final steps, and entered a long, colonnaded hall. The columns were embroidered with ivy. The ceiling was draped in chandeliers of dew. A flowering green carpet led down the hall, to a tarnished doorway. Dented and bruised, a layer of dust obscured its golden hue.

Teo pushed on the massive door. It did not budge. He dug in, pressing harder. Koda tried to help, but it was like moving a mountain. After a few pushes, he backed off. "Well, that answers that. We can't get in, either."

It took Teo a little longer to be convinced. A fury was in his eyes, and perhaps a few tears. He slammed his body against the door. In response, glittering vines slithered down from the ceiling. They coiled around and reinforced the door.

"Come on, Teo. It's locked. We need a key or something."

"I can be the key," Teo snarled. "It just needs a little more force." He walked back to the nearest column and charged the Heartwood Gate. Unfortunately, his strength rebounded against him. The door did not budge, but Teo did. He fell onto his back.

Koda rushed to help him up. "Are you alright?"

Teo swatted him away. "I'm fine." He stood up, joints cracking. He glared at the imprint his body had made on the dusty door. He chewed on his cheek, contemplating his rage. Luckily, his aches eventually overcame his anger. He muttered, "Let's go."

Koda could tell Teo was one wrong word from blowing up. So, he stayed silent while they walked back up the road. They circled the spiral highway several times before they saw anyone else. When they did, it was a lone ant resting on the side of the road. Teo snapped his fingers and beckoned it over. But word had spread that there were two boys not paying their fare. When the ant recognized them, it immediately turned away in contempt.

That set Teo off. He stormed up to the giant insect, not afraid of those venomous pincers, nor the massive sabers it had for legs. "Don't you walk away from me. You have something to say, you go and say it, you so—"

Koda grabbed Teo's arms and restrained him. The older boy wriggled free and sprinted toward the insect. Koda lunged just in time to grab him again. "It's okay. We can walk."

"This tree is huge," Teo complained in a shrill, cracking voice. He stomped his foot in frustration and put a hand over his teary eyes.

Koda had never seen the boy so distressed. He had always been confident, even a little conceited. Now, it was like they had switched places. He glanced at the sword he had been given; his reflection glinted back at him. "We walked across the grasslands, the gully, and Timbergrave. We can do this, too. Besides, someone must know about the Heartwood. We just have to ask around."

Teo glared at the ant, now proudly strolling away, and shouted something I should not repeat. But that was the end of it. He bowed his head and told Koda to lead the way.

And so, they walked—up flights of rickety rafters, across corroded catwalks, and through the Banyan's crumbling bones. While they traveled, Koda kept thinking about what Mom had said to them. He asked, "What do you think she meant by the Fisherman's Tithe?"

Teo was quiet for a moment, before mumbling in a deflated voice, "Do you really want to go home?"

Koda dodged the question, "I am tired of running from demons."

"We didn't have to run anymore. We could have stayed. We could have—" He cut himself off. "Sorry. I just liked it back there. And Mom. She was nice."

The woman had been exactly how mothers were described in books. She was stern and strong like a city has walls. Yet she was warm and inviting like a bed has blankets. Koda nodded, wondering what world awaited them if they ever left this one. "Yeah."

They eventually came to a town on the outskirts of Palimpsest. Perched on an aerial root, the buildings were all built on a crumbling patchwork of skeletal wood. Sheets of flimsy metal paved seemingly random places throughout the street. Koda and Teo walked over one of these as they entered the town. The metal cracked and bent. Koda happened to look down and to his horror, saw only empty sky for miles below. Such were the slums of Palimpsest, a hodgepodge of gashes, slashes, and amputated stems—all held together with iron band-aids.

On either side of the street, bulges and swells made hollows and hills. This gave the settlement a canyonous feeling further heightened by the stacks of shoddy shacks that lined the road. Koda squinted at the smudged signs outside each structure. This is what he saw: *Lucky Lucy's Gambling Emporium, Grim's Beverage Depot, The Saucy Spirit Saloon, Teddy's Tavern, The Monkey Bar, The Ill-Fortune Teller, Madame Monet's Palm Readings, Patrick's Pay-day Loans, Rhino Racketeering.*

"Where should we start?" Koda asked. Not that he wanted to enter any of those grimy buildings. He blinked at an unsavory spirit leaning against The Monkey Bar. Though he never moved, his shadow leaned forward and leered at them.

"How about that one?" Teo gestured at The Monkey Bar.

"Uhhh," Koda shook his head.

"Okay, fine. What about over there? That one looks promising." Teo pointed to a particularly nasty, multi-storied structure. The building in question was one Koda had not noticed, as it was on the other side of the road. As fate would have it, it was also the most infamous saloon in Palimpsest: *The Dead Man's Dirge.*

Tar dripped down the windows like molasses waterfalls, creating a sticky, shallow moat around the building. Up on the second floor, a balcony housed hulking fermentation tanks. These expanded and contracted like steel lungs and occasionally coughed up some phlegm. Rarely, the spittle would fall into one of the chimneys. Moments later the chimney would burp up the phlegm as a fireball. The saloon was elegant like a fart.

Outside, a gang of ghosts had gathered by the moat. They shared a ram's horn full of foul liquid. Imagine twice-swallowed vomit. That is how it smelled. The ghosts seemed to love it. They poured it down their empty stomachs. Koda turned to Teo, "I doubt *they* know anything about the Heartwood."

Teo stared at the ghosts and fidgeted with his canteen. "We can't know that for certain. Maybe the worst types will know the most? Some of them may even know Mahuut."

Koda did not think that was a good thing.

"How about we split up?" Teo suggested.

"That never works in movies. And I think that place is just for grownups."

Teo clicked his tongue and rolled his eyes. "Come on, kid. You think they ask for ID in the afterlife?" He joked mockingly, "Could you imagine it? *Sorry, sir. I'm afraid that you died at seventeen. Never mind the fact you died in the dark ages. Go play in the kiddie pool.*' You see how stupid that sounds? And you know, historically, most people did not live very long. They'd be turning almost everyone away! Bad for business."

Teo made so many statements in so short a time, Koda forgot about his other point altogether: that splitting up was a bad idea. And of course, *that* was Teo's point. The teenager had learned from the best. Talk quickly and confidently enough, you can make a memory forget what it was saying. So, Koda admitted, "I guess you're right."

"Course I am. Sound like a plan, then?"

Koda nodded hesitantly.

"Cool. I'll just see if anyone knows about the Heartwood. You can ask around outside. And we'll meet back here at sundown."

"At sundown. You promise?"

"Don't worry," Teo assured him, already going in. "I can be just as mean as any of these spirits." He stepped over the bubbling moat, shoved two ghosts aside, and pushed the saloon doors open.

Koda lingered in the road, unsure of his next steps. He had half a mind to follow Teo. He almost did. Then, a floating mask exited the saloon. It looked Koda in the eye and growled.

That settled it. Koda would stay outside and look into things. Preferably, without said things looking into him. He set out investigating the slums from a safe distance. After some sleuthing, he noticed a gaggle of green silhouettes. They had no bodies save for the grime and goo coating their ghostly forms. Koda listened to their conversation, but he could not make anything out. Nor could he tell how many there were. Their faint outlines were like spider webs, shifting in and out of sight depending on how the light hit them. Some were detectable only by the smoke they puffed out their invisible mouths.

Eventually, Koda figured out (from the slight variations in each silhouette) that the spirits were in a circle. Later, dice appeared on a gloomy hand. It shook them for a while, adding suspense. Then, it rolled them onto the ground and all the silhouettes leaned forward.

'*They're playing a game!*' Koda realized. He approached the circle, feeling this was a great opportunity. Perhaps if he won the game, they might give him some information.

The dice rolled to a halt. The spirits craned over them. All but one let out a groan. The winner, an oily ooze with hollow eye slits, let out a deafening roar. It widened its mouth like a snake, and one by one, slurped the losers up!

Koda blinked, mouth agape.

The swollen spirit collected the dice and noticing Koda—grinned. A gooey hand reached out, offering the dice.

He probably should have said something polite to the gluttonous ghost. A tactful, "No, thank you," might have been less insulting than just running away. Yet, his manners may be forgiven if we remember that, at that moment, Koda felt more like a piece of bacon than a human. Yet unlike a piece of bacon—he ran very fast.

Now, I wish I could tell you that this was an isolated incident, that this was the only ghost Koda fled from without a word. But alas, Koda was a child. We cannot expect such courage. Not yet.

Koda had learned nothing about the Heartwood. All he had learned concerned himself: He was an excellent sprinter and a stutterer par excellence. His sword did little to give him strength, as sweaty hands struggled to hold it.

Presently, he sat on a steel bench across from the Dirge, wondering if Teo was having better luck. He had been in the saloon for several hours. Surely, he had learned something. Yet, as the sun set, Koda was left scratching his head. Teo had still not come out. Night fell and he began to worry.

At a quarter till ten, Koda decided to get Teo.

At a quarter past ten, he entered the saloon.

A dense and damp cloud wafted within The Dirge. Koda's forehead immediately started dripping. He tried to pick out Teo from the many patrons outlined in smog. Some danced and others chugged tar at the bar. Many were also in a corner, glaring as a boy gathered poker chips into his arms.

"Better luck next time. Thank you. Who is next? Ah, Koda! Come sit down and play a round."

Koda shook his head. "The games here aren't fun." He had wanted to say more. Instead, he momentarily lost his voice. A shadow was cast behind the boy, and it was not from any light. For when candles flickered and fireplaces crackled, the shadow did not move. It lurked in stillness.

Teo did not realize this and happily slipped poker chips into his pockets. "Where ya been?" he asked casually.

Koda kept a watchful eye on the shadow as he approached the table. "Your hands are black."

"From their money," Teo chuckled. "They're all terrible sports. Imagine how awful they'd act if they ever won. But we won't let that happen, heh heh!"

Koda leaned in, "Did you learn anything about the Heartwood?"

Teo gazed at him blankly before saying, "Ah. Uh. No." He quickly added, "They're not the most talkative folks." He shuffled the cards and distributed them to the patrons at the table.

"We should get out of here," Koda whispered.

"And go where? We got nowhere to go, kid. No place to be."

Koda stepped back. There was another voice in the air, clinging to Teo's like a dissonant chord.

Teo cocked an eyebrow. "Are you scared? Look, this is just how adults operate. None of them have talked, but I'll get them to. You give me one night and I'll be speaking their language."

Koda did not doubt it and that was why he was afraid. "There's something bad in here." By that, he meant whatever was behind Teo.

"You're distracting me, kid. Why don't you wait outside? I'm sure Mom would love to give *you* a room for the night."

"Is that why you've been so angry? Because of her?"

"Course not," Teo scoffed. He took a swig from his canteen. "But I can't be thrown off my game. And if you keep pestering me, that's exactly what will happen. And then I'll lose my money. And their respect. I lose that, and none of these spirits will talk to me."

"Don't you think it would be safer to—"

"I don't care about my safety!" Teo growled. "Now get out of here before I have to care about yours!"

Koda's vocal cords pinched themselves into a futile squeak. He wished he had the courage to argue, but Teo always said just the right things to make him feel stupid.

Worse, he could not look the boy in the eye without also seeing that creeping darkness.

And as Koda left the saloon, the darkness grew.

THE FISHERMAN'S TITHE

ALL NIGHT, KODA WATCHED the door, hoping Teo would finally come out and they could leave. Yet nobody who entered the saloon seemed to come out, and Koda began dozing. The only things keeping him awake were sudden noises: rickety planks, howling wind, mysterious cackling. Though to these, he soon grew numb. When the moon was highest in the sky, he fell asleep.

Suddenly, Koda feared he had been forgotten and jolted upright. His surroundings had changed. He was in bed, back at his father's apartment. Realizing this, Koda laid back down. He pulled a scratchy, stinky sleeping bag over his body. His thrifted mattress had no bedframe, nor any blankets or sheets. It made it impossible to get comfortable. Unable to sleep, he began craving a late-night glass of milk. Or better yet, a few big gulps from the carton.

So, he got up, opened his door, and crept quietly to the kitchen. After glugging down his fill, he wiped his mouth and rubbed his eyes. The fluorescent lights flickered, nodding off at that midnight hour. They could not go to sleep, either. (Though only because if they got turned off, the roaches would invade.)

Koda peeked into the living room; it was a cluttered yet empty place. An old radio with long ears lay on the laminate. A sunken couch crouched beneath the window. Across from it was the only other piece of furniture in the room, a nightstand. It was always littered with empty, orange bottles. Koda thought it looked like a shrine. At this hour, his father usually sat on the couch, reading a cowboy book or cleaning things that did not need cleaning. Tonight, the apartment was quiet. A light came from the bathroom.

Koda thought this was strange. Cockroaches did not like the bathroom. He crept hesitantly toward the hallway. The bathroom slowly came into view. He saw his father's feet, clad as ever in combat boots. They jutted out of the doorway, motionless. His toes pointed toward the ceiling.

Koda's heart thumped, but he did not move. He reminded himself that his father fell asleep in weird places sometimes. A part of him felt like he should check on his father; another part could not bear to see him like that again.

So, the boy went back to his bedroom. He crawled into his hand-me-down mattress and wrapped himself in his sleeping bag.

Koda abruptly woke up. He had to get Teo! If the spirits in that saloon were scary, he would have to get scarier. If the shadow behind Teo was growing, he would just have to be brighter. He took out Teo's sword and stared at his glinting reflection. His determined expression left much to be desired. Namely, strength, ferocity, and what can only be described as a general unapproachability. His was not the face of a warrior.

Yet, it could be. Koda glanced at his hands, for they were the hands of a painter. And Palimpsest would be his easel.

Holding his breath, he splashed some sidewalk slush onto his face. This gave him proper blemishes and the semblance of scars. From there, he clawed at exposed chunks of Banyan bark. It had the consistency of chalk and was difficult to work with. So, Koda only used it to outline his jaw, cheeks, and forehead. Nevertheless, he produced the intended effect. The outlined bones gave him a gaunt, skeletal appearance. Finally, he dipped his finger in the Dirge's moat. Using his sword as a mirror, he added some eyeliner. It stung and puffed out his eyelids, making the final product even more striking.

Koda stared at Teo's sword, at a face of painted courage. He grinned at his reflection. It grinned back, as fierce as the foulest ghoul.

Determined, Koda darted into the street. He did not get very far, for he promptly collided with a lanky spirit. This caused them both to trip and fall onto one another.

"Oh dear, my apologies!"

Koda knew that voice. "Hermit?"

"My oh my," said the old man as he got back up. "I did not recognize you at all! You've found quite the canvas! I daresay you look positively terrifying."

"I thought you were afraid of the Banyan?"

"I was. I am. More than ever, now that I am here. But after you left, I felt like you took something of mine."

Koda searched his pockets. The old man giggled, "Oh, darn it. Forgive me, I'm still relearning my words. What I meant to say was: After you left, I realized I was missing something. Sure, the world has changed and the people in it. That does not mean I have to change with them." He cocked his eyebrow, "I used to be such a fun fellow, you know."

The boy blinked, not following the man's manic monologue.

"I've come back home." He opened his arms wide and declared, "To remember my name!" The Hermit took a deep breath of polluted air and smiled, "And I see you've got your friend's sword. I daresay it looks better on you."

"Uh, thank you."

The nameless man looked around, "And where is that temeritous fellow?"

Koda eyed *The Dead Man's Dirge*. "He went in there to get information about the Heartwood. We thought it'd help us get home."

"The Heartwood," the Hermit repeated. "What a fabulous idea! Any luck?"

Koda shook his head. "The spirits won't talk. Or Teo won't ask them. Either way, he did not want to leave."

"Oh, I know a thing or two about not wanting to leave," the old man smirked.

"It's not just that... He has a shadow."

Most adults may have brushed off that comment. *'Everyone has a shadow'* most might have said. The Hermit, however, knew exactly what that meant. His happy face darkened. "Best not waste any time, then."

They marched into the saloon just as the sun started to rise. The rays refracted on the dirty windows, causing all the patrons to glow red. Finding Teo was not difficult. He was exactly where Koda had left him. Getting back there was the real challenge. A throng of ghouls, ghosts, and ghastly gamblers had gathered around the table. All waited for a chance to beat Teo. "Pardon me," the Hermit politely said. "Excuse me. Just gonna squeeze through here. Ope, thank you. Pardon me. Sorry. Sorry."

"My friends," Teo called to them. His voice was deep and thick with overtones. "Come, watch these suckers lose." He distributed chips from his growing mountain and provided cards to the players.

"It is time to go," the Hermit ordered in a stern voice.

Teo did not even look up; but his shadow did. It loomed behind the boy, maneuvering the teenager's arms toward his canteen. Like a puppet, Teo mechanically grabbed it. His head lurched back and his jaw unclamped. He chugged the sloshing pint of putrid sludge. Then, he belched. "Who do you think you are?"

The old man stuttered because he did not know.

Teo continued, head swaying unsteadily. "Can't you see I'm getting information?"

"Look at your skin," Koda pointed. It had lost its luster and was starting to fade.

Teo stared at Koda's painted face and gave a wry smirk. He then rolled his eyes and shrugged at his arms. "Just the effects of refined sweetwater. They sell a cream for it down the street." He took another swig from his canteen and enunciated his next syllables slowly. "See? In-for-ma-tion."

"What about your eyes?" the Hermit observed. "The blue is so faded, I can see right through them."

Teo's mouth was slightly ajar. His eyes looked at the ceiling, at the headless shadow looming above him. The boy nodded to himself and stood up. "Look," he began. "I am going to find the Heartwood. But to do that, I need some more time."

The Hermit stared at the growing shadow. He whispered, "All you are doing is luring the Fisherman."

Teo scoffed, "You're paranoid."

"Do you not see the shadow?" Koda pointed.

Teo turned, catching only a glimpse before the shadow slipped out of sight. But a glimpse was enough. For a second, some color returned to Teo's eyes. He almost looked human. Almost. Then, darksome fingers cradled the boy's face. They rearranged his expression into one of pure rage. Suddenly,

Teo slammed his fists on the table and pointed a finger, "You know what? No. I've had more than enough of your whining for a lifetime!"

Koda inched away. The more he tried to help, the worse Teo got. The boy frowned. *Maybe I should leave him be?*

The Hermit stepped between them. "Do not listen, Koda. That voice is not his own."

Teo took a sip from his canteen. Black sludge dripped down his chin. "Then whose is it, old man? Hm?"

The Hermit stared at Teo; his shadow stared back. Nobody moved or spoke until, voice shaking, Koda whispered, "Mahuut."

The name echoed through the saloon. The ghostly patrons chanted it, the Hermit flinched from it, and Teo... he clasped his neck as if choking on it. He kicked as if he were swimming. At last, he turned and fully saw his shadow. But it was too late.

Mahuut reeled his catch, grabbing Teo by his thrashing feet. He untangled the fishing line from the boy's flailing arms. He removed the hook from the boy's mouth. Still dripping liquid darkness, he threw it onto the table, splashing shadows that every spirit in the saloon scrambled to lick up. They pushed Koda and the Hermit out of the way, groveling on the ground for foul droplets.

Then, in the commotion, it happened. The Fisherman raised Teo and dropped him feetfirst down his headless gullet.

The Hermit cried out and clenched his chest. He fell to his knees and curled into a fetal position. That left Koda alone, staring down the demon. He unsheathed his sword. He took a step forward. He tried to strike the spirit, as Teo had done on the river, but his arms were so heavy. He could barely hold the blade.

The headless demon walked toward them, fully revealing his foul body. Only, it was not so much a body as a collection of clouds. Clouds whose only link was the shadow they cast onto the ground. Body parts wafted and recombined. Fingers fell off his hands; shoulders slid to take their place. Arms sank to become legs. Legs became arms. And his chest...

His chest expanded. Mahuut inhaled. A chill wind entered the saloon. It snuffed out the candles. It stole the fireplace's flame. It even took the reflection in Koda's sword. All the light went to Mahuut, who enveloped it. Then, his chest deflated. The light he had stolen was exhaled as foul orbs. The patrons of the saloon chased after the orbs. Like fish in a frenzy, they gulped them down. It took all Koda's strength not to do the same.

The Headless Fisherman stared at him and chuckled. "You proved the more resilient. I should congratulate you. As for your friend, be troubled. For the boy and I are one." With a flick of his wrist, curtains fell and covered the windows. The saloon went pitch black. Koda felt as if he were underwater—like the pressure of a thousand fathoms bore down on him. He could not breathe.

The Hermit staggered to his feet, choking. He grabbed Koda's arm and pulled him through the throng. How they managed to find their way out of the Dirge, only miracles know. Yet find their way they did, running into the street and collapsing to their knees. They gasped in the filthy air, thankful for anything to breathe.

"Are you okay, Koda?"

The child did not answer, for he had looked up at the sky. What he saw made him tremble. A foul cloud in the shape of a canoe floated overhead. Mahuut stood proud on the prow. In the giant's chest, exactly where a heart should have been, was a boy in fetal position. Ghostly oars rowed away, and a dirge came from the clouds. It was sung to the tune of *Heave, Ho. Heave, Ho.*

REAWAKENING

THE NIGHTMARE WENT THE way it always had. Koda tried to stop it. He pinched his dream self a dozen times. The nightmare was ruthless, though. There would be no waking early. This time, it would conclude. It did so while Koda was sheathed in his sleeping bag. And try as he might to cover his ears, he heard those haunting words as clearly as the day they were uttered.

"An hour sooner and he might have made it," said the first paramedic.

"What do we tell the kid?"

"Not that."

"Then what?"

"I don't know. That his father died peacefully in his sleep last night?"

Koda awoke in the lower bunk of a familiar bed. He had no idea how long he had been asleep. From the crust on his eyes, he guessed it had been a while. He glanced to his side. The Hermit sat half-asleep in a green chair embroidered with golden leaves. He noticed Koda was awake and nearly spilled the cup of cold tea in his hand. "Ah! You're awake! Sleep well?"

Koda shook his head. Everything after the Dirge was a blur. "How did we get back here?"

"I brought you," he replied. "Carried you, actually. No, no. Don't apologize. And don't be embarrassed! I was glad to do it. Though I admit, I took a few wrong turns along the way."

Koda touched his face. His skin was smoother than it had been.

"I also scrubbed all that stuff off," the Hermit explained. "Didn't want you to break out."

The boy nodded slowly, too confused to be thankful. "How'd you know where this was? We were probably on the other side of the Banyan."

At that, Mom entered the room. She held a vase of freshly cut flowers. "He and I are old friends."

The Hermit added, bowing his head gratefully, "For many years, this was the closest thing I had to a home."

"Oh." Koda asked the caretaker, "Do you know his name?"

She put the flowers on the desk next to the bed. "He forgot it long before we met."

The Hermit's knees began to bounce. "Yes, well. Anyway." He frowned at Koda, "I wish I had come sooner. What bad luck!"

Mom put a hand on the Hermit's arm, "We cannot say what is good or bad luck."

"Teo was fine until he went inside one of their restaurants." Koda sat up, "He was just supposed to ask about the Heartwood."

"Maybe he did," said Mom with a shrug.

Koda stared at her because that was an obviously stupid thing to say. Still, he kept calm and quiet. Then, the Hermit told him it was going to be alright. That annoyed him. "People only say that when things are *not* alright."

"That's true, I suppose." The Hermit momentarily looked out the window before abruptly shooting to his feet and declaring, "I'll make us some tea. I brought my set." He fled to the kitchen.

Koda watched Mom mosey through the room. She picked up stray pieces of trash, pocketed them, and inspected the dresser. She opened and closed the first two drawers before taking Koda's clothes from the third. She set them on the desk and stated, "We'll get your friend back."

Koda bent his legs so that his knees guarded his chest. "No, we won't. He's gone. I saw him in Mahuut's belly."

Mom sat at the foot of the bed and eyed Koda's duffel bag. "We'll think of something."

The boy sat there, looking at his lap. Then, like the kettle beginning to boil in the kitchen, his anger bubbled up. "He abandoned me."

Mom frowned. As with tea that is still too hot to drink, she let the child be.

A moment later, a clang came from the kitchen. Shortly after, the Hermit reappeared upstairs. "Tea is steeping. Though, might I bother you for a broom? I dropped a cup."

Mom told him to sit.

"But—" the old man blinked. He glanced at Koda, saw he was angry, and looked away. "It's a green, you know? Don't want it to be too hot, it might make—Oh, I suppose there are bigger problems than bitterness." He sat across from Mom and Koda. His legs bounced anxiously.

Koda wanted to keep quiet as a form of protest. Though, he had no idea what he was protesting. After a minute of staunch resistance (to nothing), he muttered, "Mahuut said they were one now. What does that even mean?"

"Mahuut is a liar," said the matron of the house.

Koda stared blankly, "Or, he's a goner."

"So was I," the Hermit acknowledged. "And you saved me."

Koda's voice cracked and he shook his head, almost laughing. "What? No, no I didn't."

"Sure you did," the old man stated. "You were the one who told me I could make this trip, that these old bones still had some use."

Koda had not said all that. However, it is often the little things one says that have the most impact. That was the case now. Koda had only pointed out that the Hermit had gone past his porch. It was a polite suggestion, a soft nudge. Yet so long had the Hermit been alone, all he needed was a nudge.

"You were different," Koda argued. Aside from the hermit, the last people he had tried to help had wound up eaten, petrified, and worse. He curled himself tighter into a ball. "Teo doesn't want help."

"You would abandon your friend for that?" Mom asked. "For not wanting help?"

After some hesitation, Koda nodded.

"What a bad friend," she declared.

Koda had been accustomed to the woman's softness. He was not prepared for her harshness. He looked at her and she sternly stared back. Her gaze became a spell from which Koda could not break. He could not bow his head. He could not even blink. So, he wrapped his arms around his legs, shrouding his heart evermore. "I'm not a bad friend. I tried to help. It made it worse."

Mom said nothing. That was all she needed to say.

Koda's coldness melted away. He felt incredibly dumb. Further, he felt like an awful person. Those two sentiments combined into an overwhelming self-loathing that, like a sneeze that will not come out—infuriated him. Finally, he unlocked his arms and lowered his legs. His heart was thumping so hard, he was sure people saw it.

He spoke with a creaking, unhinged voice. "What if I only do more harm?"

"That might happen," Mom admitted. "Like accidentally uprooting a flower when you pull a weed."

Koda spoke with immense shame. In time, he would understand why. For now, he carried her metaphor forward. "I'd rather have both than no flower at all."

"But you do not have both," the caretaker noted.

Koda's lips quivered. He had left Teo alone with the demon. "I—I should have gone in with him. I should have been there. I abandoned him."

"Ssh." Mom scooted toward Koda and opened her arms to him. Koda crumbled. He coiled into a tight hug and balled into her chest. Meanwhile, Mom gently threaded her fingers through his tangled hair. "It's going to be alright. And you better believe that."

"How can I?" Koda cried. "You weren't there. You didn't see what happened. I abandoned him."

Mom gently rocked Koda, "Where is there?"

The question was innocently asked. But perhaps you also see what she was getting at by asking it. Koda did too, and that is why he did not answer—at least, not directly. "I should have checked on him sooner."

"You cannot stop what you do not start. His actions were not because of your inaction."

Koda began to panic. Every breath brought less air into his lungs. He started hyperventilating.

In response, Mom took a deep breath. Time slowed. The rising of her chest became like a wave to driftwood. When she inhaled, so did Koda. When she exhaled, so did Koda. In and out. In and out.

His panic passed as quickly as it came. Koda sat up and wiped his eyes. It was dark outside. No sunlight could break through the greenish clouds. It should have been dark in the room—darker than the outside at least. And yet, Mom was her own light. She made the room glow. And when she put her hand on Koda's shoulder, her smile was kindling. It burned away the dead wood of the past.

Koda knew what needed to happen. He looked at the Hermit, then at Mom. "Where does Mahuut live?"

Mom stared out the window, "Mahuut is a nomad. His home is the hearts of those he has corrupted."

Koda followed her gaze. Swirling clouds swam through the air like a school of fish. Somewhere in the polluted sky, Mahuut was watching him. He gulped his fear and declared. "Well, I'm a nomad, too. I'll find him."

"I do not think that will be necessary," Mom said, squinting at the pollution. "In fact, I think he will come right to you."

"How?" Koda asked. "I'm not going to be like Teo. I won't drink that gross stuff like he did."

"I'm not asking you to."

"Then how can I lure Mahuut?"

Mom's answer was simple. "The Ancient One."

"Hey!" exclaimed the Hermit. He eyed them both before realizing what the woman meant. He gasped, "Wait. You found a true Ancient?"

"And perhaps if we wake him," Mom suggested. "He might know how to get into the Heartwood."

"What about Teo?" the Hermit inquired.

Mom elaborated, "Mahuut hungers to see the Heartwood. It is the last pure place he has not polluted. If the way is opened, he will not be able to resist. He will come right to us."

Koda sat up straighter. "Why didn't you say all this before?"

"Because I had not thought of it," Mom replied. She stood up. "Now if you're feeling up to it, the Hermit's tea has steeped long enough."

The Ancient was in the Solarium. Perched on a tall pot, Alfalfa's roots had cracked the clay and spread across the room. They were now starting to dig into the floor. Yet, they were no longer a silky white but a sickly black—the same sort they had seen in Timbergrave.

"Alfalfa," Koda reached out hesitantly. The spirit's head had retreated almost entirely into the seedpod. "You feeling better?"

The Ancient stirred slightly.

"Please, we need your help. These two think you can enter the Heartwood." Koda turned toward the others and groaned, "He's a tree. He doesn't talk!"

The Hermit put on his bifocals. "Of course he does. That's a blessed being. If we cannot hear him that is our own fault." The old man walked carefully around the spirit's overgrown roots. He put a hand on the Ancient's seedpod. "I don't suppose you remember an older boy. Teo was his name."

Silence.

"He has been taken," continued the Hermit. "And I know it might be hard to believe, but you could be the key to rescuing him. But to do that, we must expose the Heartwood to Mahuut. Are you willing to do this? Are you willing to face the Headless Fisherman? The Barbarian of the Banyan?"

The seedling's roots began to slowly slither. For a moment, the Ancient seemed to be emerging. Then, the roots dug deeper into the ground and entrenched themselves in the foundation.

"Please, Ancient One. The evil creature that took your home also took our..." The Hermit trailed off, remembering something. He scrunched his face in confusion. Then, he took a deep breath and sat beside the seedling. "Look, I know a thing or two about not wanting to move. I know how scary it is to face a fear. I'll tell you something, though. It is better to face one's shadow than hide from it in the dark. Trust me on that."

Silence.

"We should give him a moment," the old man suggested.

"He's had enough of those!" Koda shouted. He turned his anger toward the Ancient. "What kind of seedling needs all these roots? Do you want to be like this forever?!"

Mom began to leave, "We cannot force someone to act." She turned and peered at Koda. There was a magic in the way she could look at you. From her eyes alone she could tell you something. In that moment, she was telling Koda to be patient. Only days ago, he was doing precisely what the little seedling was doing.

And so, they waited.

The trio gathered in the drawing room and talked over tea. Some of the other residents were drawn out of their rooms and sat around to listen. Others observed from the loft. They were a kinder sort, each with some sickness that made them incompatible with the rest of society. Some were too wise, others too slow. Some could not rest, some only knew how to dream. None cared for Mahuut.

They talked for hours, mostly about little things. You might call it small talk, but for the spirits in the sanatorium, such trivial words were like medicine. Everyone was especially interested in the Hermit's story. They were shocked that a spirit could simply leave the Banyan and were saddened to learn it did not make him happy.

Koda did not say much. For a while, he stared at his reflection in Teo's sword. Then, he grabbed a chair and sat beside the fire. He watched the flames shift, a one-man theater troupe constantly putting on new faces. As he watched the dancing fire, he thought about the Fisherman's words. What had he meant about being one with Teo? He asked suddenly, "Who is Mahuut?"

The other spirits hushed. Some left the room altogether. But there was one spirit, alone in the solarium, which now began to listen.

The Hermit began the tale: "Mahuut was once a wanderer, like you. The Ancients left him alone because he did not care about knowledge. They thought this made him spiritually gifted, but in reality—it was the opposite."

"You see, Mahuut loved the thrill of fishing. He was always hoping he might catch the biggest fish. It was an obsession that only grew as he wandered. He went to ponds and took all the guppies. He used them as bait in the rivers. Then, he caught all the trout in the rivers. He used them as bait in the oceans. He caught marlins, sharks, even whales—and yet, he was never satisfied."

The Hermit shivered and bowed his head. Koda turned around and waited for him to go on, but the old man would say no more. The spirit in the solarium began to stir.

Mom picked up where the Hermit left off. "After emptying the oceans, he realized that *he* was the biggest fish. If he were to catch anything worthy of his dreams, he would have to use himself as bait."

The Hermit interrupted with disgust, "He chopped his own head off! Attached it like a lure to his line! That was when the Ancients knew they had been deceived. By then, it was too late. He cast the bait into the Banyan's boughs, creating a feeding frenzy of lesser spirits. They gathered around the grotesque head and began to gorge. Yet, as they feasted, Mahuut's rotten head grinned. For he had hooked the whole world."

Koda stared at the old man's hands. They had lost their age spots, wrinkles, and scars. Nonetheless, they tremored—aftershocks of some ancient earthquake. Like his body, the man's voice quaked. "He desecrated the sacred home and turned its hallowed mother into a pauper!"

"I remain as rich as ever," Mom corrected proudly. Her eyes glanced toward the kitchen, where the cabinets had begun to shake. Glassware was ringing to a crescendo.

The Hermit went on, lost in blind hatred. "He traded his humanity to become a beast. A monster!"

A pot fell off a shelf. A pipe burst beneath a sink.

The Hermit glared at his hands, "All to sate his hunger for a single day!"

The floorboards winced and whined. Tension rippled through the walls. The earth groaned below them. The remaining spirits looked at one another and fled to their rooms. That left the trio to bear witness as the foundation heaved.

The seconds that followed were the quietest of Koda's life. They ended with a crash that shook the entire house. Dust and debris shot into the drawing room. Shingles, bricks, and broken glass exploded into the kitchen.

Stunned, everyone looked around. The only one who did not seem disturbed was Mom, who finally got that broom the Hermit had asked for. She calmly gave it to him and gestured toward the kitchen. The Hermit took it and walked warily toward the commotion. He disappeared into the kitchen, tiptoed through the mess, and gasped when he entered the solarium. He ran back to them and announced, "The Ancient One has awoken!"

Division to Addition

THAT WAS THE LAST day of Palimpsest. And though Koda could not have known it then, it was also the first. A big reason now loomed above them. Burst from his shell (and the roof), Alpha had grown into a great tree. Massive trunks were clad in a mossy kilt. Broad arms bore thorny gauntlets. A lichenous beard swayed above a bark breastplate. In place of a lonely leaf was a garland crown, resting proudly on the Ancient's head.

"I'd almost forgotten what they look like," the Hermit remarked.

"Not me," Mom said. "And they never looked quite as kingly as this one."

The great spirit nodded at her and lowered a hulking arm. He unfurled his armored hand, beckoning them on.

The Hermit was the first to take the offer, saying, "I walked in your kind's shadows as a child. And though I may not remember the name my mother gave me, I know that name rang clearest in your forests."

Koda's heart raced. His adrenaline made him jittery. He was enraptured by the grandeur and power his friend now possessed. But he was also afraid. Sorrow and fear had left the little seedling; that was evident. They were cast off like the shattered shell of his seedpod. In their place was a new emotion, one which Koda liked even less.

Realizing he may need it soon, Koda gripped the hilt of Teo's sword. However, just before he walked atop the Ancient's hand, Mom stepped in front of him, knelt, and clasped the boy's shoulders. "Remember, it is not the fault of a tree that it drinks polluted water."

Koda did not understand her meaning until long after that day. Still, he knew she was saying something important and gave her a determined nod. He joined the Hermit on the treeish hand, which placed them atop the crowned head. Like reins, they held onto the garland as Alpha let out a deafening roar.

So began the march to the Heartwood. They strode across the causeways slow and strong. When the winds blew, it was from the Ancient's breath. When the Earth trembled, it was from his footfalls. And with every step, the once-frail seedling seemed to grow even larger. Koda had never seen such strength before. This was no gun or sword, no epic hero from one of his father's movies. This was violence itself.

No spirit, foul or friendly, dared look upon them. The not-so-giant ants hurried off the highway. The oozing monsters scrambled out of sight. Thirsty spirits across the city hid in their saloons. Within minutes, not one poltergeist in Palimpsest on the path remained. When the Ancient raised its leg, the air held its breath. When its foot fell, the wind howled and fled.

They descended the spiraling highway. The Ancient destroyed any dwellings in its way. It smashed the shanties and toppled the treasure dens. The wasps and the wisps, the ghosts and the ghouls—every pest was purged from Palimpsest.

Then, at last—they reached the bottom and came to the colonnaded hall. All was quiet there, as it had been for many years. Yet, it was far colder than Koda remembered. As they went, he also noticed the ivy leaves had brown tips. The dew chandeliers had all dripped dry. The sap sconces were dim and faint.

The lumbering Ancient approached the Heartwood gate. The golden door glimmered through its layer of dust, though only in the places Koda and Teo had touched. The Ancient placed its hand upon the entrance. The columns quivered and gilded dust fell onto their heads. Slowly, the interlaced and bejeweled vines around the gate began to un-coil. The door shuddered and opened. A stagnant, old wind blew out of the inner chamber.

A silver reflection pool glittered as if from moonlight. It smelled like the sweetwater river. Alpha entered the pool, which was not deep. The water sloshed back and forth in its basin. Then, for a moment, all was still.

Slowly, buds formed on Alpha's garland crown. The buds swelled and burst into a rainbow of blossoms. Yet as quickly as they came, they fell into the water, replaced by a thick layer of leaves. These too did not last long and fell also into the pool. On and on this cycle went, with the Ancient's garland springing to life only to fall.

Koda worried the pool would overflow with fallen leaves, yet it never did. The debris disintegrated rapidly into twin-kling specks that made Koda wary of touching the water. The Hermit had no such fears and climbed down. Once he had been in the water for a few seconds, Koda followed. The old man helped him down.

Their stomachs growled. Neither had realized how fam-ished they were. They bent down and scooped up a handful of sweetwater. Koda took only a little sip at first, expecting it to be bitter. Fortunately, it was just as juicy as the first time. He was tempted to get a second handful but knew better than to keep drinking. The boy turned to see the Hermit's reaction to the water. Yet the old man did not like the taste. He wore a worried look and wandered to the pool's perimeter.

Strange figures surrounded the basin. They were not seedlings or saplings. These were men and boys. Some were old, even older than the Hermit. Some were barely toddlers. Yet whether they stood with hunched backs or crawled on all fours—all were turned to stone. Some had fearful faces laced with sorrow; some were entombed in anger. No matter the differences, they all had one thing in common—especially the older figures.

The Hermit brushed his fingers along a stone watcher's face. He turned to Koda, eyes wide and scared. The boy looked at the man, then the statue, and gasped, "He looks like you."

The Hermit nodded, unable to say anything. He walked to another statue. This one wore a sun hat and had discolorations on his cheeks. The figure wielded a pitchfork and carried a sack behind him. "If I had been a farmer, I might have looked like him, too."

Koda inspected another watcher whose head was bowed. He could not see the face properly, but the nose and cheeks looked familiar. "This one has a long coat."

"A lab coat," the old man corrected. "See the chest pockets and the name tag?"

Koda saw both. The name tag was smudged. He walked to the next watcher in the circle, then the next, and so on. Every statue had something that made it unique. A couple held big stacks of books and had bespectacled faces. A few carried tool belts and hauled hefty equipment. One even looked like a soldier and carried a weapon. No matter their occupation, they all stared through veiled eyes with a look of unhappiness.

Koda recognized that look. He recognized the faces, too. Some belonged to the Hermit, varying only slightly: a scar here, a different haircut there. But the younger ones, the middle-aged adults, looked like someone else. They looked like Koda's father. Now, staring at the Hermit from across the twinkling pool, Koda remembered his first impression of the old man. He had looked like his grandfather.

Koda had a hundred things to say. He interrupted himself a dozen times. He managed a handful of words. "Mister, are these you?"

The man reflected on his face in the water, "Of course not." He pointed at the soldier statue, "I was too frail to be a soldier. And too rowdy." He gestured at the scientist in the lab coat, "And I never had the smarts for science, though I liked it." He bowed his head and a lone tear fell into the pool.

The Ancient stirred.

Koda went to one of the youngest statues. It had a mask on and was set in a theatrical pose. He asked, "Did you ever want to be an actor?"

The Hermit was silent for a long while. "I wanted to be a lot of things. For other people. For myself. But who we want to *be* is not who we really *are*." Suddenly, he gasped. For sometimes, a thing may be said that says a lot more than the thing. Sometimes, a simple sentence can be a key that unlocks a hidden door. To a memory long forgotten.

"What is it?"

The old man went stiff. He fell onto his knees, causing a ripple in the water. Then, he grabbed his head in horror.

Koda rushed to help. "D—Mister?"

The old man turned and gazed with terror. A black smoke seeped out of the old man's eyes, clouding them. He whispered, hoarsely, "I've remembered my name."

The reflection pool began to bubble. From the Hermit's tears came a shadow. It grew quickly, taking shape as a slinking silhouette. The old man collapsed and it took a rasping breath.

"Mahuut," said Koda, taking a step toward the exit.

The Headless Fisherman turned and stared at him, but he was no longer headless. Fixed like a fleshy jack-o-lantern was Teo's expressionless face.

"Teo!" Koda screamed.

"The boy is gone. As is the old fool." Mahuut laughed, "They were gone long before you began your meddling."

Koda reached for Teo's sword.

Mahuut glided toward him. Teo's blank face declared in a monotone, "It is high time to pay your tithe. What form shall your payment take?" Mahuut's dusken claws coiled and tapped the water. The ripples produced images of terrible things—bottles and blades, worries and wraiths. The demon smiled and the ripples formed a single image. Orange pill bottles glowed like candles beneath the water.

Koda trembled, bound in place by the demon's will. A fog of thick smoke rose and obscured the hall. He was trapped.

A sickly fishing pole floated up from the floor. Mahuut grabbed it and fixed an orange bottle onto the hook. Within the bottle was a beckoning face, a minuscule monster made for Koda alone. I will not tell you what the boy saw, for I do not know. All I can say is it tempted him. The boy's mouth watered.

The demon flicked his wrist and cast the line just in front of Koda. An intoxicating scent sent a comforting sensation through his spine. A powerful nostalgia crippled him and took over his mind. He bent forward to take the bottle. All was almost lost.

But there are sacred places that never suffer shadows. There is strength that cannot be surrendered. And in those waters, there was still a pure reflection. Seeing his face gazing up at him, Koda covered his nose and his mouth. With all his willpower, he slashed the lure with his sword, severing it from the line.

Mahuut hissed and reeled the line back in. He removed the bottled monster and tossed it into the water, where it promptly dissolved. He conjured a new lure: a woman. He cast her at Koda's feet.

The boy could not resist looking. He glanced at the conjured creature and was confused. It resembled Mom. Moreover, it wore a subtle, lavender perfume which brought back memories he did not know he had, of happy times in a country house. The woman extended her hand.

Koda might have taken it. He certainly crept closer. At first, he just wanted to make sure he was seeing correctly. Then, he wanted to see if her skin was soft. Maybe even get a hug. He reached out, but he never got the chance to touch her.

A huge hand crashed down onto the Fisherman's hook. Waves washed away the trick. When Koda wiped his eyes, now free of the spell, the woman had dissolved. Between him and the Fisherman now stood a proud and angry Ancient.

"Alpha!" Koda cheered.

Mahuut roared, "I had hoped to put you in a zoo, you pest." His pole sizzled and burst into flames. From the fire emerged a smoldering harpoon gun. "I will fuel my furnaces with your bones."

And so they sparred, the Demon of the Waters and the Last Seed of Timbergrave. The sylvan spirit smashed, swiped, and stomped. Mahuut evaded the blows and, between assaults, prepared his own. After dodging a hulking hand, he launched his harpoon. It pierced the Ancient's chest, searing the wooden flesh. The Ancient doused itself in sweetwater and snapped the harpoon in two.

Mahuut began to cast a new spell. Black flames slithered out of his hands and into his harpoon gun. He aimed and fired a flaming web. It flew and coiled around the Ancient. A hundred holes were burned into its body. Smoke billowed up its pockmarked bark. Enraged by the pain, it barreled toward the Fisherman. This caught Mahuut off guard. So much so, Teo's expressionless face showed signs of life.

"Teo!" Koda yelled.

Mahuut hastily reloaded his harpoon gun. Rather than dodge the incoming blow, he knelt and waited. Blinded by hate, the Ancient thundered directly into the harpoon, impaling itself. A barb went through its throat, but not before two great fists slammed into the Fisherman.

All went quiet. All was still.

Slowly and with great struggle, the Ancient lifted its arms and wrapped its hands around the burning weapon. With a groan, it ripped the barb from its neck and stumbled backward. Sap flowed from the wound as it baled water onto its flaming body.

Meanwhile, Koda rushed over to Mahuut, whose shadow had shrunk. Teo lay beneath the darkness, wrapped in its black blanket. Some color had returned to his face. The boy blinked at him. "That you, kid?"

He tried to say something; hulking legs thudded behind him. Heavy arms creaked. The Ancient roared. Koda turned to face the raging spirit. It glared at him, body still burning and mind still seething. "You won, Alpha. Look! Mahuut is crushed. And look, it's Teo." Koda glanced at the boy, whose blue eyes were regaining color. "You remember Teo, right?"

It was no use. Fury takes time to dissipate. In trees, it takes centuries. And this particular tree had been angry for many, many years. The Ancient was deaf to Koda's pleas. It raised its mountainous leg.

His sword arm shook; his legs did not. Koda stood his ground.

"Get out of the way, kid," Teo rasped. "I deserve this."

"No!" Koda yelled. He lifted his arms, protecting Mahuut's broken shadow. He held his breath as the massive trunk hammered down.

Just then, the Hermit shouted something. Roused moments ago by Teo's reemergence, he rushed toward the children. He pushed Koda out of the way and grabbed Teo. Yet, pulling the boy from the shadow was like pulling himself toward it. He fell forward, and they were both crushed beneath the Banyan's foot.

Immediately, the air turned hot. Koda peered up from the edge of the pool. The water began to simmer and bubble. In seconds, it was in a full boil. The Ancient retreated from the steaming pool, revealing the remains of the victims. Or, rather, the remains of *a victim*. For in the center of the Heartwood lay a single body.

THE PAINTED FLOWER

THE WALLS OF THE Heartwood had fallen, and feathery starlight floated from the naked sky. The Banyan's branches—thick with bricks, chimneys, and steel—had collapsed. The horizon was clear and empty. Sunlight pierced the smog, scattering it.

Koda sat up. A familiar tree stood before him. "Alpha?" he asked, fearful that the Ancient was still enraged. The spirit did not move. Eventually, Koda approached. He reached out and touched the tree. The spirit began to turn its head, but Koda would not live the lifetimes necessary to see it. Instead, he looked down at the Ancient's legs. They had been sewn into a single trunk, though a hole had appeared at the bottom. Koda squatted and peered inside. A fox nestled snugly around its kits.

Koda searched for his friends. He walked through the meadow and climbed ruinous mounds. He surveyed the rubble, rubbish, and all. Teo and the Hermit were nowhere to be found. He turned around, about to give up. As he did, he noticed a figure standing on a cliff.

Koda called out, "Hello! Teo? Mister?"

The person did not respond, so Koda hiked up the cliff. He came to a ridgeline that overlooked the new Banyan. The person, a man in his forties, was staring down at the meadow. The sun was high in the sky and yet, this stranger did not have a shadow. Nothing did. Koda crept closer to the man.

He had a random patch of white on otherwise brown hair. He wore old-timey glasses and had black combat boots on. They looked worn and ready to be thrown out.

Koda gulped. His heart began to beat irregularly.

"Now this," said the man softly. "This is a hill made for sunrises." He inhaled as if it were the first time he had done so. He exhaled as if he had held his breath all his life.

Koda took a step closer. "Dad?"

The man turned and smiled, "Hey, kid."

Koda's eyes got full and watery. He raised his empty hands.

His father clicked his tongue and winked. "Don't worry." He took the white urn out of his pocket and placed it beside him on the cliff. "You picked a good spot."

"You died," Koda whispered.

His father sighed, slowly shaking his head. "I died long before you were born." He knelt, putting an arm around his son's shoulders. "But now I can live. Thanks to you... You did more to heal my spirit than I ever did."

That should have been enough to forgive his father. In time, perhaps it would be. For now, forgiveness stayed mute. Koda mumbled only an, "Okay." Then, he blinked at the urn, the little white container he had lost on the train. "I don't understand."

He patted Koda's back, walked to the cliff's edge, and turned. "You will." He adjusted his glasses and smiled. "And now that we've had a proper goodbye, you must excuse me. I have an old friend to find."

He disappeared into the wind.

MY FRIEND, TEO

KODA AWOKE IN A hospital room. A string of flowers hung above his head. At the foot of the bed was the familiar face of Agent Wellington. She had a few scrapes on her and looked very tired. She gave him a pleasant look and asked him something. He did not hear her and sat up.

"Easy, Koda. You had a serious concussion."

"What?" He asked. Had he been dreaming all this time? He looked for his father's ashes and was distraught when he could not see them.

"It's gone, Koda. I'm sorry. The river took it." Wellington was bruised and her bun was completely undone. She sighed and looked out the window. "The conductor was..." the agent thought to spare him the details. "He had too many adult beverages."

Koda clarified, "So he was drunk."

"M'yes." She cleared her throat, "Fortunately, nobody was hurt too badly."

Koda stared at his surroundings in a daze. *'Nothing was real?'* he asked himself.

"I'll go talk with the charge nurse and see if we can't get you to your mother's house today."

"My—my what?" Koda thought he heard her wrong.

"Your mother." She added quickly, "She was the one who was supposed to be sitting here, not me."

"Then why isn't she here?" He had asked that question many times before.

"Well, the thing is. Something has happened at your mother's house." She licked the inside of her lips. "I guess it's quite a mess right now. She couldn't get out of the driveway."

"What happened?" He pressed. This sounded like one of his father's convenient stories—what some folks might call a fib.

"To be honest with you, Koda, I'd rather us just go and see for ourselves." It was clear from her tone; she too thought a lie or two was being told.

Koda's head was starting to hurt and not from the concussion. He watched Agent Wellington leave like pictures in a slideshow. As soon as she left, he got up. His clothes had mostly dried and were draped over the visitors' chairs. After slipping on his hoodie, he noticed it felt oddly heavy. Something was in the pocket. He reached in and was shocked to feel sleek, cold plastic. He pulled the strange item out and gasped. It was a tube of titanium white—the same paint the Hermit had given him.

When the nurses came back, they found Koda standing there, touching his face in a daze. They immediately made him sit back down, do a few tests, and sign some papers. (You might remember, adults make you sign things to do anything. They even make you sign papers to be alive.)

Outside the hospital, the city was oddly comforting. Like a fog that burns away by the afternoon, the dull greys of the city seemed to have lifted. Koda now saw the little details in the brick, the lichens and the moss. He noticed the weeds in the sidewalk cracks and looked all around at the windows of shops and apartments. He saw his face in a thousand glass panes, a thousand blank canvases, and was comforted.

There were no trains running that day. As such, they took a taxi. Koda leaned over to his caseworker and commented, "She lives in the country. This is going to cost a lot."

"It's not my money," said the caseworker, flashing a card. She got in the backseat of the taxi and patted the seat next to her.

They left the city in silence. Koda could tell the taxi driver wanted to ask what had happened to them. He kept looking at their bruises from his rearview mirror. Thankfully, the driver was polite and left his passengers alone.

After an hour, the car left the pavement and began bouncing down a country road. They passed the river first, then a field of wheat that stretched on for a long while. The road followed a dry riverbed that soon wound through a thicket of trees. Made up of maple, apple, elder, and juniper—all were a sickly brown.

Another hour passed with bumpy roads, dust clouds, and frail, weeping trees. By the time they turned down a new road, they were in a barren forest of bony branches. Not one leaf grew in the thicket. Not one leaf.

Yet, as Koda dozed off—he saw a green mailbox. It was unremarkable in every way except for one: It marked a change in the surroundings. Everything beyond the mailbox was alive and green. Things grew so thickly, it was impossible to tell when one tree started and another began. It was all one canopy.

The cab slowed. The taxi driver turned, "Can't get ya any further."

Wellington woke from a nap and exclaimed, "Oh, my!" Blocking the road was a fallen tree, the largest Koda had ever seen. It was skeletal white and had died long before it had fallen. Prairie dogs sat atop it in a row, legs hanging lazily off the edge. They looked like construction workers on lunch.

When Wellington stepped out, the prairie dogs chirped at her, saying something in their own language. They shuffled off in an organized line, leaving her befuddled. "What in all creation? Right, okay. Come out this way, Koda. Just scoot. Yep. There we go." She leaned into the cab, "Just wait here a minute while I drop him off. Okay?"

"Not too long," the driver replied. "It is getting late and this road is a little... under the weather."

That was an understatement. The fallen tree had left debris all over the road. It made the rest of the journey feel like a hike. They climbed over roots and ducked beneath low-hanging branches. They stepped over prickly weeds and slid over slippery moss. Koda was glad he had no toys to carry around.

"I was just here last week." Wellington pointed at a surface root. Dry, cracked dirt looked as though it had been recently pushed up. "This road was in rough shape. Nothing like this, though."

Passing an overgrown hedge, they entered a courtyard. It was encircled by maple trees. At the center was an old Victorian home with a proud porch and sky-blue siding. The red shingles were worn yet elegant.

Wellington ruffled his hair playfully. "Let's get you inside. Your mother will be—oh, well look at that. She's waiting for you."

Koda squinted. He had not seen the woman since he was very young or at least—that is what he thought. Yet the woman perched on the porch, sitting in a wheelchair, looked exactly like... Well, like Mom! And the house was exactly like Mom's Sanatorium. It was identical, down to the faded white paint and the chipped, red door.

Koda would have hesitated no matter what, as he had not seen his mother in so long. Now, though—he hesitated because he *had* seen her. Just the other day! He walked slowly up the steps, staring at the woman. He did not blink, because she would definitely disappear if he did. He touched her arm, just to make sure she was real.

The woman wept. Koda pulled away.

"Don't do that," she said in Mom's same, soft voice. "These are good tears."

Koda came back to her nervously.

She wiped her eyes and put her hands on his cheeks. She got a proper look at him—cried some more—and then wheeled herself around. "You must be famished!"

Koda blinked at her. He managed a slight nod.

"Make yourself at home in the drawing room," she said, opening the front door. "I'll make some tea. We have so much to catch up on!"

He repeated as she rolled away, "The drawing room?"

"The living room," she told him. "Just inside. I call it that because it sounds better. Makes it seem fancier. And before you ask—yes, you can draw in it. Just not on the furniture like you used to!" She laughed herself off to the kitchen.

Koda entered his mother's home and sure enough, he recognized it. There was the wallpaper and the fireplace, the curvy couches with ferns woven into the fabric. But there were also things he did not recognize: mementos on the mantle, knick-knacks on the walls, photo albums on the coffee table.

Koda sat on the couch and kicked his legs for a while. Remembering the paint in his hoodie pocket, he took out the tube. He fidgeted with it, tossing it from hand to hand. Then, lazily and without much intent, he twisted the cap. It opened.

Koda gasped and looked down. He dabbed a bit of white on his finger and analyzed it. It twinkled like no paint he had ever seen, like starlight in liquid form. And the twinkles were not just glimmers of the same white, oh no! In the right light there was red, green, and everything in between. With the proper canvas, any color might well come out!

Koda capped the paint, wiped his finger on his sleeve, and put the tube back in his pocket. His mother was talking with his caseworker in the kitchen.

"When did that tree fall?"

"If I told you the truth," his mother answered softly, "You'd think I was crazy."

"I dealt with Koda's father," the caseworker said flatly.

That elicited a faint chuckle. "Fine. Well, that tree had been dead for years. I always liked it."

"Storm knock it down?"

"Nope. It was a perfectly sunny day. No wind. Nothing. It just fell over."

"Really?"

"Mhm. And here's the strange part. It fell right after you called."

"About the train?"

"Not a second after I hung up the phone."

"Well, that's weird." A long silence punctuated the conversation. Then, the caseworker continued, "I'll see if I can call in a favor. Get someone up here and clear the road for you."

"You don't need to do that."

"That's true," Miss Wellington agreed. "I'm still going to do it, though."

Koda thought he heard a tissue rip. "Thank you, Natalie." The women whispered a few things he could not hear. A few seconds later, two thumps against someone's back signaled they had hugged (and that the hug was now over). Agent Wellington came out of the kitchen, wiping her eyes. Beaming at him, she knelt. "I'm going to go, Koda."

He asked, trying to sound like he did not care, "You're not going to stay?"

That only made his caseworker cry more. She took a staccato breath and composed herself. "Not with the way the road is."

"Oh," Koda said, trying not to sound disappointed.

Wellington offered him open arms. "Can I get a hug?"

"Is that in your job description?" Koda inquired, unable to hide his grin.

"Not at all," she chuckled.

Koda shrugged and hugged her. It was a longer hug than was necessary for someone just being nice.

His caseworker commented, "Careful, Koda. People might start thinking you are kind."

"I am kind."

"Yes. Yes, you are." She patted his back and smiled down at him. "I'll be back in a week to check on you two."

"Okay," Koda replied. He had the urge to say a few more words. But, as he had not yet said them to his mother, he refrained.

After Wellington left, his mother continued clanging away in the kitchen. Koda was alone in the drawing room for a long while. So, he opened one of the photo albums and began flipping through the pages. Most of the photos were of his mother, of him, or the two of them together. His time with his mother was like a fog lifting away with the flipping of every page. Koda felt sad about how much he had forgotten. It was like all his mind and memory had been devoted to his father, of whom the photobook had not even a rumor.

Then came the last picture in the album.

A boy in black and white smiled from the page. Koda's first thought was that he looked like Teo, though not as wild. His second thought was that the boy had definitely been bullied, as he wore circular glasses that made his eyes look huge. Additionally, his T-shirt was tucked in and his lanky arms were far too long for his body.

But one of those arms was wrapped around a huge, smiling dog. Koda had never seen one so big before. He did not even know they got that big. He did know, however, that nobody would dare bully someone with a dog like *that*.

"Ah," said his mother as she entered the room. "I love that album." She set their cups on coasters, lifted herself off the wheelchair, and sat next to him.

"Who is this?" Koda asked, though he had a guess.

"That's the only picture I kept of your father," she replied.

Koda looked at her, confused.

His mother took a deep breath. "Your father had his problems. He wasn't all bad, though. He loved animals. Did you know that? Well, he did. At least, when he was a boy." She pointed at the dog in the picture, "He loved that dog more than anything. When your father found him as a stray puppy, he was already as big as you! But he had too big of a heart and died suddenly. Just after this picture was taken."

"I think a part of your father died that day," his mother continued. "Because he always talked about that dog. Said it was his guardian angel. And I won't throw away a picture of an angel."

Koda wished he had a dog like that. He immediately frowned and wagered they would be very expensive, or too difficult to handle. He asked, "What was the dog's name?"

"Teo."

ALSO BY

Ah, and now we've come to it—the end of the book! I hope that if you have made it this far, you enjoyed this story. If you did not, I commend your perseverance! Regardless of whether you thought it was a classic piece of literature or a piece of something else altogether, please consider leaving a review on Amazon, Goodreads, or wherever else you buy your books. (If you buy your books in person, feel free to scream about the book as you walk down the street.)

The support and *honest* feedback of readers is the most important thing for independent authors. We do not have the luxury of corporate executives telling us our writing sucks. We depend on the charity of our readers for that.

I recommend a palate cleanser after my novels. Something stylistically different or easy to read, like Dr. Seuss or The Bible. If, however, you are not weary of my writing style, below are some novels for your consideration.

The Innkeeper and the Cannibal

The Forlorn Trail: Book 1 of the Eye of Ur

Teo and the Banyan Tree